HER PERFECT LIFE

EMILY SHINER

INKUBATOR
BOOKS

Published by Inkubator Books
www.inkubatorbooks.com

ISBN (eBook): 978-1-915275-68-4
ISBN (Paperback): 978-1-915275-69-1
ISBN (Hardback): 978-1-915275-70-7

PROLOGUE
MILLIE

WEDNESDAY

My hands ache from gripping the shovel handle, but I take a deep breath and scoop one more bit of dirt onto the soft mound before letting the tool drop from my hands. Carefully, I step onto the soft mound and stamp it down, moving slowly.

My new shoes are filthy, but the mud doesn't matter, not when there's already blood on one. I'll have to throw them away, have to buy new ones. The last thing I want is for anyone to see me out and about wearing dirty shoes.

Eve wouldn't have, so I can't.

When the ground is flat, I step back a few yards and lift my hand up to my eyes, to shield them from the sun. It's late in the afternoon, and the sun has reached into the woods where I'm standing; the rays warm my face as I examine the flattened area of dirt.

"That simply won't do," I say.

Eve talks like that, says *simply* a lot, because she likes the way it rolls off her tongue. I've always thought the word was ridiculous, but I can start getting used to saying it.

I raked a pile of leaves to the side of the grave earlier. Now I swap the shovel for the rake and pull them back, trying to make the site appear messy and natural and not like I fiddled with the leaves to make them look like they hadn't been staged. Some of the bottom leaves are wet, and when I'm finished, it's obvious that I was digging around in the dirt here.

But maybe after a day, nobody will notice.

Maybe, as long as I play my part, nobody will even come looking for her.

My back hurts. I stretch it out, putting my hands on my hips and slowly bending over, to work out the muscles there before I pick up the shovel and rake. The last thing I want is to leave any tools out here where someone might find them.

It's silly, but I feel like I should say some words. We were twins, after all, practically inseparable throughout childhood, only growing apart when we got older and realized how different we actually were.

I brush some hair back from my face. It's a bit shorter than Eve's, but I can easily explain it, say I got a trim. More than I hate the length, I detest her blonde dye job. Still, it's a lot better than the alternative, of having to live out the rest of my life as me.

"You were my sister," I say, keeping my voice low. There isn't anyone else out here, but I keep quiet anyway, to make sure nobody passing by accidentally overhears me. I'm alone, I'm sure of it, but you can never be too careful.

"You were my sister," I repeat, unsure of what else to say. What would I say to Eve if she were standing next to me, waiting to hear what I had to say about her? What words would come to mind if I didn't know she was buried a few feet below me, already less beautiful than she was—her perfect tan and manicured nails hidden from the world?

I know. I know what I'd say.

If she were alive and standing in front of me, waiting to hear what I thought, waiting for some kind of sisterly wisdom and love, I know exactly what I would say to her.

"You deserve this."

The shovel and rake are heavy as I carry them, but my steps feel lighter than before on the walk back to her house.

No.

My house.

1

MILLIE

WEDNESDAY
Two Weeks Earlier

The sun is so bright when I step outside, I have to stop and close my eyes so I don't lose my balance. Sure, I felt the sun on my face before, but not for a long time, and I can't describe how overwhelming it feels right now.

"Are you okay?" The man asking that isn't checking because he's worried about me; he wants me off the property before I have an episode. If I were to pass out here or get dizzy and need medical care, then he would have to alert someone, and they'd have to bring me back inside.

The Lynchburg Correctional Facility is glad to be rid of me.

"I'm fine." I swat my hand in his direction even though he didn't reach out to offer his support. "I just need to get used to the sun on my face."

He snorts, and I'm sure it's because he's thinking of all the time I spent out in the yard with the other prisoners. What he doesn't understand, and what he probably never will, is that the sun inside the yard isn't that bright. When you look up at the sky and see barbed wire around the perimeter, obscuring your view, it's not the same.

Outside the prison walls, the sky appears to stretch on forever. Inside, the sun is locked in a tiny box, so all you see is a sliver of the sky, an unnatural shape that you can't quite make sense of. Even when you try to drink in the view, you're always aware of the hulking building behind you. In here, your entire life revolves around other people's schedules; you never get to do anything without their permission.

I keep my back to the prison and give my head a little shake, to clear away my thoughts, when a car pulls up to the sidewalk and stops, its engine idling.

"This you?" The guard almost seems surprised, like he can't believe someone would come for me.

"It's me."

I ignore his curt tone, ignore the fact that it's not my sister sitting in the driver's seat, ignore that I had to call an Uber to get out of here. I pick up my bag and walk quickly to the waiting car.

The driver rolls down the back window a little, just enough for me to look inside. "Millie Grant?"

"That's me."

"Great."

The driver looks way too young. He has dark circles under his eyes and an earring in one lobe. The earring looks ridiculous, but what do I know? I was in prison long enough to miss out on the latest trends and fads.

I hop in the back of the car, throwing my bag in first, then slam the door shut. The last thing I want is to spend any more time at the prison. This part of my life is over.

And I have huge plans for the next part.

"Where are you going?"

"Chadwick Heights, number 137. It's at the end of the street, in a cul-de-sac."

The driver pulls away from the curb, and I settle back in the seat, looking out the window at the prison. As the building grows smaller and smaller, I finally feel the tight feeling in my chest start to relax.

For the entire morning, I kept expecting someone to come to me and tell me they'd made a mistake. I thought for sure they would take away my clothes, take away my bag and my shoes, and put me back in the same outfit I wore for the past ten years. I couldn't sleep last night thinking about it, and now that we're finally driving away, I'm beginning to think this isn't a joke.

I look down at the bag at my feet. It's made of clear plastic, so everyone in the prison can see what you have with you. I'm wearing the same clothes I had on when I was taken to jail, only this time they fit differently.

They're too big. In the last ten years, I lost weight and gained muscle. I did everything right, kept my head down, made sure I didn't upset anyone in the yard.

And during every moment of free time, I studied. I had to get out of prison, had to prove my innocence. I worked hard, poring over law books and case law, talking with my lawyer weekly until he got sick of me and told me to find someone else to help me.

So I did. I found an organization that works with people who were wrongfully convicted. They helped me, guided me, made sure I was on the right page every time I cracked open a law book. And then, when we got my conviction overturned, they wanted to plaster my face all over the news.

And I said no.

It would have been amazing, wouldn't it, to see myself in

the paper and on news reports and to know that people finally learned the truth about me? From the beginning, I wanted to rub it in my sister's face, to prove to her that I wasn't a murderer. But over time, that goal changed.

They say that people find religion in prison. I always thought that was ridiculous. Why would you turn to something that you have no control over when your life is already out of your control? I didn't want peace. I wanted revenge.

That fueled me for the first five years until I grew tired of wanting revenge. After my obsession faded, I realized how tired I was of the constant dreams about hurting my sister. I wanted out. Instead of focusing on her, I poured all of my energy into getting out of prison and getting my life back.

I went to chapel. I met with the chaplain. We prayed; we talked. I raged at first, crying over how I was treated, but then I got over that. I forgave my sister for what she did to me, even though that seems almost impossible to believe.

And now I'm free.

I just want this nightmare to be over. I want to look my sister in the eyes and ask her why she did what she did. I want to find the closure that I deserve.

She at least owes me that much.

2

MILLIE

WEDNESDAY

I wish more than anything that the prison had given me something other than a clear plastic bag for my belongings. The cheap handles cut into my hand as I stand on my sister's front walk. My Uber driver offered to stay behind until I was sure someone was home, but I waved him away.

This is going to work out.

I forgive Eve for what she did to me, and now I want to look her in the eyes and tell her that. I want to hear her apology, that she did the wrong thing, that she's sorry, that she would take it back if she could.

She knows she's untouchable. Before I went to prison, the police suspected her of killing Joe. Detectives ripped her house apart looking for proof.

Her alibi? Airtight.

Her house? Spotless.

Her reputation? Amazing.

Taking a deep breath, I hurry up the front walk and pause on the porch for a moment before ringing the bell. I always loved this house and thought that Eve would move out after Joe died, but she didn't. Instead, she settled in even more, enjoying the life that was stolen from me.

The doorbell is so loud that I hear it over the pounding of my heart. I give it thirty seconds before I start to shift my feet uncomfortably.

What if she isn't home?

The columns on the front porch feel like two sentries guarding the property. I feel my throat close shut. This is the same feeling I got in prison whenever it was time to come in from the yard. Glancing over my shoulder, I look up at the broad sky, reminding myself I'm out. I'm free.

But the question now is how long do I wait for Eve to answer?

Before I can decide, my sister throws the door open. Her eyes widen when she sees me on her front porch. I open my mouth to greet her, but she takes a step back and grabs her chest, like she can't believe what she sees.

"Millie?" My name is a combination of a swear and a prayer on her lips. I close my eyes, letting the word wash over me.

It's been years since I heard her say my name. We're so different, but that doesn't mean I don't love her. How could I not? Even after what she did, I forgive her. I fought like hell to be able to stand here. She's my twin.

We shared a crib. We dressed the same all through middle school. There's a flicker of anger in the back of my mind when I think about what she did to me, but I extinguish it, breathing deeply like the chaplain taught me.

"What are you doing here? Are you going to hurt me?" Eve has both hands on the door, ready to slam it in my face.

"No," I say, holding up one hand. "No, I'm not here to hurt

you, Eve. I wanted to come by, let you know that I'm out of prison."

She glances past me down the street, and I wonder if she's looking to see if her neighbors are watching.

Or if the police are on their way.

"How did you get out?" She still hasn't moved. Her knuckles are turning white from how hard she's gripping the door. She stares at me, her eyes wide, her cheeks visibly pale under her tan. "Nobody told me you were getting out."

I shrug, a little embarrassed by how this is going. "They found me innocent, and I got out and came right here. Can I come in and talk to you?"

"No." Her body stiffens. She looks me up and down, finally letting her eyes settle on my face. "No, you may not. How can I know why you're really here? You could be here to hurt me."

"I'm not. I forgive you, Eve. You did this to me, but I found religion in prison. I'm not mad. I just want to talk to you."

It feels like I'm floating above my body and watching this interaction. I see how calm I am, how patient.

I also see how angry my sister is.

"No." She spits the word at me, and I actually wince. "No, I'm not talking to you. You killed Joe. You shouldn't be here."

"I didn't kill Joe." I frown at her. "Please, I just want to come in and talk. Is that too much to ask?"

Eve straightens her back a little and is silent for a moment, giving me time to study her. I weighed more than she did when I went to prison, but a terrible diet and ten years of walking and lifting weights took care of that. Her hair has blonde highlights and is set in a high ponytail. Her huge diamond earrings sparkle in the light.

I take in her yoga pants, the expensive logo on her tank top, her French manicure. We were mirror images of each other when we were younger.

Not anymore.

In contrast to her I feel dumpy. My ten-year-old clothes are too big, but even if they did fit me like they were tailor-made, the jeans and cardigan don't show off my shape like her clothes do. I never had a tan, never had my nails done.

We're twins, but I can't help thinking that Eve and I look like a before and after picture that you might find in a celebrity magazine.

"Eve," I say, but even as I speak my twin's name, I know she's going to shake her head—and she does.

"No, Millie, no. I don't want you to come in. I don't want you to be a part of my life. There's nothing between us, you have to realize that." She glances past me again, then peers at something down the street.

My jaw drops open as I realize something; the back of my neck prickles. *Is someone watching us?*

Feeling anxious, I look over my shoulder at the house across the cul-de-sac, but I don't see any movement over there. I honestly don't think I could handle knowing that someone was watching my sister turn me away like this.

"I'm not angry—"

"I am," Eve says, cutting me off. "You killed Joe."

I frown. "No, if you listened to me, you'd know that I didn't. They found me innocent, Eve." I lean in, lowering my voice. "I know who killed Joe, just like you know. But it's okay. It took a lot of work, and I was angry at first, but I forgive you."

I thought she'd be cordial when seeing me, would at least invite me in. I thought we'd talk about everything over tea. That's never going to happen, and it's clear to me now. There was no way she was going to let me into her house, not when she's the reason I was in prison at all.

"I don't know what you're talking about," she says stiffly, "but if you don't leave, I'll call the police."

My blood runs cold at the thought. I can't go back to prison. I can't sit in a windowless room across from a detective who already believes that I'm guilty, just so my sister can have some peace and quiet in her life. I did that, lived that hell, and I promised myself I wouldn't ever go through it again.

"You know I went to jail for you."

She scoffs, lightly touching her throat. She has a tennis bracelet on, one I hadn't noticed before. The diamonds sparkle as much as the ones in her earrings do, and I have a sudden urge to rip it from her wrist and throw it on the ground.

"You went to jail because I'm smarter than you," she says. "Because I was able to see what the police saw—that you're a murderer." She closes her eyes for a moment, taking a deep breath before looking back at me.

I feel anger rising in me, the same anger that I tried to leave behind me years ago when I stood in the prison chapel and asked God to forgive me for hating my sister. For wanting to hurt her. For thinking every moment about what I would do to her once I got out. I turned my life over to Him, for whatever that's worth.

It's not like I had much of a life in the first place to turn over.

"I went to jail because you framed me." She doesn't answer, so I continue. "You called me over to your house, told me you needed to talk to me. I came, because that's what I always did for you, Eve, but you weren't here. As soon as I left, someone killed Joe and called the police, putting me at the crime scene. You think that I don't know what you did? I want us to sit down and talk and—"

"We're not having this conversation. You and me?" She points at herself, then jabs her finger at me in an accusatory way. "There *is* no us. We're over."

My stomach clenches as I think about how this should have gone, how I dreamed this would go. "You're my twin—"

"Was your twin. I *was* your twin until you killed my husband."

Now it's my turn to close my eyes. I count to ten slowly, doing my best to calm down the way my counselor showed me. She believed in me. She promised me that everything would be okay once I got out.

She was wrong.

She didn't know that Eve framed me for Joe's murder. I can't prove it, the police couldn't prove it, but that doesn't mean it didn't happen. I know she killed him.

"I didn't kill him, Eve. You know that. You know what you did to me, what you took from me."

Eve smiles.

My voice is getting high and tight, and I want to smack the smile off her face. "You know you did this. You took my life from me."

She laughs, the sound too bright and saccharine. "You had nothing for me to take, Millie. Don't act like prison was that big a loss for you."

Before I can respond, she slams the door in my face. It shakes on its hinges, and I listen as I hear her engage the locks.

One.

Two.

Three.

What in the world is my sister hiding from that she needs three locks?

3

EVE

WEDNESDAY

Millie is out of prison.

Those five words send chills up my spine. I try to push them away, try to ignore the growing sense of dread in the pit of my stomach, but it's impossible.

She's out of prison. She came to my house. I'm pretty sure I did a good job making it clear that she isn't welcome here, but how am I supposed to know for sure?

I pace the floor, my feet eating up space before I stop, turn, and go back. My nerves feel frazzled, and the hairs on the back of my neck are sticking up.

No, she wasn't a killer when I had her sent to prison for killing Joe. She was good, innocent—pure. A little naive, perhaps, but that's not who she is anymore. The fact that she came to my house under the guise of wanting to talk has me worried.

There's no way that after so many years in jail she would want to be friends. No way in hell.

"She found religion," I mutter to myself. "Bullshit."

She's up to something, I'm sure of it, but I don't know what it is. I have no way of knowing what she's trying to do, and I just have to try to stay safe.

My phone rings, and I fumble it out of my pocket. Relief floods through me when I see the number on the caller ID is not Gareth's. The last thing I want is to hear from him. He wouldn't understand that I'm worried about my sister right now. That, or he wouldn't care. My life is only a game to him, and the last thing he'll want to hear about is my concerns over my twin.

Gareth has been playing with my life for years, and while it's never come back to hurt him, I'm afraid of what will happen to me if something goes wrong.

Like if Millie does something stupid.

Or when he gets scared.

I answer the call.

"Mrs. Overstreet? This is Detective Lee. I want to let you know that your sister is out of prison. She had her conviction overturned yesterday. I highly doubt that she'll come by your house, but you need to be aware that it's a possibility she might show up."

The detective's voice is familiar, considering all the times we talked about the case.

I swallow, ready to cut him off. "Detective, I appreciate your call, but Millie has already been by here."

He's silent, and I'm sure he's thinking hard about what I just said, looking for a sensible explanation. I'd love if he could explain it, because Millie showing up on my front porch after so many years isn't something I ever thought would happen.

"Are you okay?" I hear him shift position like he's getting out of his chair, getting ready to come here and protect me. "Did she threaten you?"

I recall how she looked standing on my front porch. "No, she didn't. I know it's going to sound crazy, but she actually wanted to talk to me, said she forgave me."

The words are out of my mouth before I can stop them; it's too much to hope the detective didn't hear them.

"Forgave you? For what?"

Sweat trickles down the back of my neck. *For framing her for Joe's murder.*

"For not ever coming to see her in prison, I guess. I mean, what was I supposed to do, try to have a relationship with the woman who was convicted of killing my husband?" I force a chuckle to show how ridiculous the thought is. "No, there wasn't any way I could do that. I think that's why she came by. She wanted to... let me know how she felt. Let me know that she forgave me even though she had been angry at me while still behind bars."

"And did you two talk?"

"No. The last thing I want is for her to be in my life. I don't care what the courts said; there's no way she didn't kill Joe. I told her she wasn't welcome here, and she left." Anger washes over me, and I close my eyes, fighting it back. It's one thing to be angry at Millie but another to reveal to this detective exactly how I feel.

Still, I hate her for showing up here, for thinking everything is fine.

For thinking we could ever have a relationship.

For somehow managing to convince the courts she's innocent. I knew it was a possibility, of course. It always is, no matter how hard you plan and how careful you are when setting someone up. But never did I think it would happen to me.

I worked really hard to keep that from happening.

Detective Lee exhales hard. "If she comes back around and makes you feel uncomfortable, I want you to give me a call, do you understand? We can't let this continue."

"I don't think she will," I say, "but I'll let you know. Thanks so much for the call, Detective. I appreciate you looking out for me and letting me know she is back on the streets."

He pauses, and for a moment I think he's hung up, but then he clears his throat. "For what it's worth, there are some detectives here who don't think she's innocent. Me included."

Another pause follows, and I realize how tightly I'm gripping the phone. Before I can speak, he continues, "The evidence was too perfect. We don't see crimes like that. Because we can't charge her again due to the double jeopardy rule, that makes her much more dangerous. Be very careful if you think she's coming after you."

"I do. I will. Thank you."

Before he can say anything else, I hang up the phone. As much as I appreciate him calling to let me know about Millie, that news ship has sailed. She had the guts to show up on my front porch in the middle of the day when anyone could see her. I hate that she thinks she has access to me.

I hate that she thinks she can come to the house and everything will be fine.

She wants me to know that she forgives me, but she can't know for certain how far I actually went to get her thrown in jail. It wasn't something that one day crossed my mind and I jumped on it before I had a chance to think things through. No, I was smarter than that. I worked a lot harder to make sure things worked out the way they were supposed to.

And now what the hell am I going to do?

I debate calling for help. The thought is appealing, and I

let it rest for a moment, drumming my fingers on the
while I think it over. There's one person I could c
would be able to take care of my little Millie proble... once
and for all, but I don't want to go down that path.

So far I've managed to avoid becoming a suspect for the
murder of my husband, but now that Millie is out of prison, I
don't know how much longer that protection is going to last.
Detective Lee said it himself just now—there are still people
who think Millie did it. I didn't think much of his comment,
but now that I think about it, there may be more to his
statement.

What if he was issuing a warning—that some people
think Millie did it, but others don't? Was he implying that I
might be a suspect?

I can only imagine the upset among some detectives if the
case fell apart. The evidence points directly to Millie, so of
course some of them will keep believing that she murdered
Joe.

How many times did I go over the case and the evidence
in my mind? It was airtight. I was so careful with everything,
but maybe that was a bad thing. It never occurred to me that
the crime could be *too* perfect, but what do I know?

I thought having everything clearly point to Millie would
make the case go smoothly for me, and it did, but maybe the
detective was right. Perhaps no murder case wraps up that
easily.

A chill runs up my spine as I contemplate what that
might mean for me. Millie's been cleared of the crime, which
means the detectives are going to start looking for the real
killer. I covered my tracks, I know I did.

But what if someone uncovers them?

Wrapping my arms around my body, I try to shake off the
chill. There's no way the police think that I had anything to

do with Joe's death. If they did, they'd be at my door right now. I wouldn't be at home, worried about what might happen if the police dig deeper. I wouldn't be nervous about who might show up at my door.

I certainly wouldn't be wondering what the hell I'm going to do about Millie.

4

MILLIE

WEDNESDAY

I sit down on the edge of the sagging bed and drop my head into my hands. Rubbing my temples, I try to rid them of the throbbing feeling, but I can't shake it.

This is not how I thought my reunion with Eve would go.

I was never so deluded to think she would throw her door and her arms open and welcome me back into her life, but I also never thought she would slam the door on me, deny what she did, continue to spin the same lies she spun for the police.

"God, I need to get out of here."

It's the first time I've prayed since leaving that razor-wired world. The words don't feel as comforting as they did when I was still in prison.

On the inside, the words were weighted; each one felt heavy. I rolled them around in my mouth while I prayed, enjoying the power they gave me whenever I used them. But now the words feel light, powerless, almost invisible.

I try again. "I don't know what to do, God. I have to figure out how to live in the same world as Eve. I wanted her to talk to me. I thought maybe an apology might mean she understood what I've been through." I pause, listening.

It's not that I ever heard God speaking, not in the way you hear your cellmate talking in the middle of the night, but in the past I was able to *feel* something.

I was able to feel less alone. That someone is with me even though I'm the only one lying on my cot.

I remember all the times I went into the chapel and prayed, the many times I talked to the chaplain about how I was going to get out and try to reconnect with Eve. I forgive her. I know I shouldn't. I know most people in my position wouldn't.

When I first went to prison, I was so angry, so ready to lash out at anyone who got too close. I wanted to hurt Eve, wanted to make her feel the pain that I felt when she turned on me and framed me for Joe's murder. But anger like that will eat at you, so I forgive her.

Well, I forgave her before she closed the door on me. I'm not sure I do any longer.

My hands clench into fists at my sides when I remember her gripping the door, staring at me like it was a surprise to see me again, her face white with shock, her body dripping in expensive jewels.

I went to prison for her, I forgave her for it, and what was she doing? Living her best life, enjoying the finest things that life had to offer. I suffered, was scared a lot of the time, and I worked my ass off to prove that I was innocent, and what was she doing?

Pilates and tanning from the looks of it.

"How am I supposed to forgive her?"

I wait, my eyes still clenched shut, my breathing shallow. I need an answer from God. I need to feel that deep calm settle on me again, like it did when I prayed in prison. I got so used to the feeling that someone heard me, to feeling that I'm not alone, and now that is gone.

"What?" I whisper the word. My stomach tight, I stand up. "Why isn't it working?"

Forcing myself to take a deep breath, I close my eyes again, then drop to my knees.

There. This is how I always prayed when I was in prison. On my knees, in the dirt, begging for forgiveness for all the things I wanted to do to Eve.

A knock on the front door interrupts my thoughts. I push up from the floor and brush my dark hair out of my face as I walk over to open it.

It has to be my sister. She followed me here to apologize, to tell me that she's sorry about how she acted, that she actually does want to sit and talk.

Plastering a smile on my face, I throw open the door, only to have it slide off a moment later.

"Large pepperoni with extra cheese?" The woman standing in front of me holds the pizza on her palm like a waitress in a fancy restaurant and pops her gum at me while she waits. "Ma'am? That'll be $13.59."

"Right. The pizza. I'm sorry, hold on." Leaving the door open, I go to my plastic bag and dig through it until I find my purse. I pull it out. My credit cards are all expired. Luckily for me, I had enough cash on hand to pay for this hotel room for two weeks and order in some food.

I press a ten and a five into the woman's hand. She glances down at the money.

"I'm sorry I don't have more for a tip," I tell her, taking the pizza from her. "But I hope you have a great day."

"Having a great day won't pay the bills." She sniffs at me

like I personally offended her, but then she wheels around and hurries back to her car. It's an old hatchback with a Jimmy's Pizza magnet stuck on the side.

I watch her go, then lock the door and sink onto the bed, opening the box to grab a slice. Sure, there was pizza in prison once a month, but it was nothing like what you can get on the outside. The cheese was always greasy and congealed, the meats slightly gray in appearance.

This pizza looks just how I remembered. My mouth waters as I take my first bite.

"Oh, God, that's good," I say, and then it hits me what I said.

I keep calling for God, but he's not answering. I'm completely alone out here. Even my sister, the woman who screwed me over in the first place, whose life I protected by going to prison for her, doesn't want me in her life.

Flopping back onto the bed, I keep eating, trying to imagine what her life was like without me. I'm sure she has friends and lots of things to do during the day. I bet she works out and goes to the salon regularly.

Rolling over, I grab another slice. I can't even remember the last time I went to a salon. Getting your hair cut in prison is nothing like getting your hair cut at the nice place down the street where they offer you a glass of wine while you wait.

"Must be nice," I mutter to myself. "Must be nice to have such a wonderful life when mine was an absolute shambles for so many years. I wonder what nice is like."

As I eat my second slice of pizza slowly, savoring the flavors, I think about what to do next.

Tomorrow, when I feel more grounded, I can figure out what to do about more permanent lodging. The bank was more than happy to take my house after I was convicted, and although there's plenty of money sitting in a frozen bank account, I don't have anywhere to live.

It's not that I thought Eve would offer to move me in with her, but I'd be lying if I said that I didn't hope it would happen. Not that I would want to, of course. It's one thing to forgive the woman who framed me for her husband's murder; it's another entirely to move in with her.

But she could have offered to help me get back on my feet.

She has everything. Her life is a dream, but only because she ruined mine. If she hadn't killed Joe, hadn't framed me... where would she be?

I'm not sure, but what I know is that I wouldn't be where I am now. I wouldn't have just gotten out of jail for a crime I didn't commit.

I went to see her to let her know that I forgive her, but that's not what I want anymore.

I want what she has.

I was in hell. Locked away. Forgotten.

And for that entire time, Eve was living her best life.

Now it's my time.

Not just to live my best life, but to live hers.

5

MILLIE

THURSDAY

"I'm so sorry, ma'am, but I'm not going to be able to accept your driver's license. It's expired." The teller talking to me shifts her feet, obviously uncomfortable having this conversation with me.

I can tell she's embarrassed for me.

"I've been out of the country." I feel my cheeks grow hot with the lie, but I soldier on. "It's not like I could pop out to the DMV to get it taken care of when it came up for renewal."

"I understand," the teller says, but the way she looks at me tells me that she sees right through my lie. "But I hope you can understand that these accounts are frozen, and I can't let you access the funds until you produce a valid ID." She slides my expired driver's license across the counter to me and taps it with one long, manicured fingernail. "It can be a state-issued ID, if that's what you can get. It doesn't have to be a driver's license."

"Thank you anyway," I mutter, grabbing the card and slipping it into my purse. While I was talking to her, a line formed behind us. I avert my eyes as I walk out of the bank, not wanting to look at anyone. I still have some cash in my wallet, but taking the bus or an Uber everywhere is quickly eating up my funds.

"Okay, Millie, think. What are you going to do?"

I stand outside the bank, my arms wrapped around my chest, as I watch the cars speed past. The bank is on a busy corner downtown, right across the street from a little restaurant that wasn't there before I was incarcerated.

I would have remembered a place called Blue Sky. It's cute but bourgeois, and I'm not surprised to see the parking lot full of hip, electric cars.

A sleek black car pulls in, and I watch as a tall blonde gets out and shuts the door with her hip. She's talking on the phone and casually beeps her key fob over her shoulder before glancing around the parking lot. Skinny jeans meet impossibly tall high heels with red soles. Her loose-necked sweater exposes her shoulders, but she doesn't seem to notice the chill that I do.

My blood runs cold.

Eve.

She doesn't see me staring. Or if she does, her eyes flick right past me like I'm not here. I dig my nails into my palms and have to catch my breath when she walks up to the entrance. In a moment, she's gone.

I came up with my plan to deal with Eve late last night, but there are a few things I have to do before I can take over her life. We always looked identical growing up, but while I'm pale and brunette, she's tanned and blonde—a combination I can only imagine is more costly than I can afford right now.

I'm halfway across the street before I realize where my

feet are taking me. I open the door to the restaurant. There's a little bell above the door that jingles cheerily. I shut the door quickly to keep the gust of cold wind out of the restaurant.

"Hi, just one today?" A hostess with a button nose and freckles grins at me. She's holding a menu in her hand.

I smile at her and glance around the room, searching for my sister.

There she is. By the far windows. She's at a table for two. Two glasses of iced tea are already poured. Her knee jiggles as she waits.

I could go over there and sit down across from her, but I don't want to. She had her chance for the two of us to talk. That ship has sailed.

"Yes, thanks, but it's cold by the windows. Do you think I could sit at the bar and get something to drink there?" I gesture vaguely toward the bar, to a spot that gives me a clear view of where Eve is currently sitting, with her back to it.

"Sure, sounds great. Just a drink, then?" The hostess drops the menu back onto the main pile and motions for me to follow her.

"Just a drink," I confirm, keeping my head turned away slightly as I walk past Eve's table. I notice her whole body is tight and turned to the window, like she's unable to keep from looking out there. As we walk by her, I turn and scan the parking lot to see what she is checking for.

I see nothing but nice cars. Whatever or whomever my sister is waiting for hasn't arrived yet.

"Here you go." The hostess rests her hand on the back of one barstool. "Enjoy."

I nod, taking in the sights and sounds around me. Maybe it was a mistake to come in here. The noises are louder than they were in prison, the lights brighter. It's like I'm absorbing both. I'm forced to take a deep breath before I pull out the barstool to sit down. The seat is covered in rich green leather, and I run my fingers across it before finally sitting down.

As soon as I'm settled, the bartender walks over. He throws a towel over his shoulder and grins. "Hey, you look like you need a drink. Something strong, perhaps?"

I shake my head. Maybe in the past I could drink something strong, but I haven't had alcohol since the night Eve framed me for Joe's murder. For the longest time, I worried that the rum I drank that night could have had something to do with what happened.

I wondered if I'd had so much to drink that I forgot I killed him.

I wondered a lot of things.

"Nothing strong," I say, thinking quickly. "Coffee with Baileys?"

He arches an eyebrow at me, then gives me a nod and makes it. When he puts my hot drink down in front of me, I take a sip and then turn to look at Eve. The only thing I can see from here is her perky ponytail and how she's tapping her fingers on the table. Whomever she's waiting on still hasn't shown up.

Taking a deep breath, I turn back around and pick up my cup. It's not fine china by any means, but the little filigree pattern around the lip is pretty. I run my finger across it. It's not clumsy and heavy, like the mugs in prison were.

Everything there is built to be sturdy, even the people. You go in weak and desperate and come out strong. That's what I did.

The chatter from diners is overwhelming. I feel like I'm crawling out of my skin, and I know I need to get out of here fast, get back to my crappy hotel where it's quiet and I can at least think things through.

Half an hour. I'll give it half an hour, and if nothing exciting happens by then, I'll leave.

The coffee is hot and delicious, and I close my eyes as I let the flavor linger on my tongue. It's nice to slow down and enjoy a drink even though it was probably silly to follow Eve in here.

Even a simple coffee with Baileys is sure to cost an arm and a leg in a posh place like this. It's an indulgence, that's for sure, but I need it.

Mostly, though, I want to see what my sister is up to.

When I glance down at my watch, I'm surprised to see that I've only been here five minutes. It feels like hours. The noise from the restaurant has changed from a dull roar into something that's almost ear-splitting.

Thirty minutes. I promised myself I could do thirty minutes, but when I check my watch every minute for the next five, I know I need to leave sooner.

Half an hour isn't long. I told myself I could do it, but I'm having doubts. If I don't get out of here, I'm not sure what I'm going to do. Everything is too loud, too bright; there are too many people.

I place some cash on the bar and cast one more glance at my sister before weaving through the tables. She's still alone, still jiggling her leg like that's going to calm her down and make her more comfortable. I don't approach her.

She had her chance.

The restaurant is only a few blocks from the hotel where I'm staying, and I head that way. But first, I stop at a gas station to buy a cell phone. I'm running out of cash, and quickly, but tomorrow morning I'll go to the DMV to get an ID. As soon as I have that, I'll be able to get my money from the bank.

I need the money, not only so I can move out of the hotel, but so I can also dye my hair. Get a tan. Go shopping for a few more clothes. I don't care if most of them are not my style—

laid-back and comfortable. I'll need at least one pair of heels to make this work.

Plus one tight pair of yoga jeans. Plus a cute sweater that shows off how thin and in shape I got in prison.

I look like my twin, but not enough.

Not yet anyway.

6

GARETH

THURSDAY

Eve always has this terrible habit of bouncing her knee up and down whenever she's nervous or upset. It's a dead giveaway, and one I warned her about the first time we met. But it's like every bad habit.

Difficult to break.

I know why she's nervous, just like I know why she wanted to meet me in a public place. She wants to put this behind us, to move on from the agreement we made, but I'm not that type of person. When you agree to help me, you don't get to back out. I show up a little late to our meeting. It probably gave her false hope that she had a way out, but that wasn't why I was late.

I really wanted to watch her squirm.

She stirs her iced tea and takes a sip, her perfectly stained lips leaving a smudge of lipstick on the straw. When I sit down, she glances at me, hope and fear written across her face.

"I was thinking," she says, tapping the table in time with her bouncing knee, "that maybe we could amend our agreement."

"Amend it?" Linking my hands together, I lean forward across the table to get a better look at her.

She shifts back a little. Her eyes dart from side to side, like she's afraid of who might see us talking.

"How do you think we should do that?"

"I want out." She whispers the words, then covers her mouth like they weren't supposed to be said out loud. When I don't respond, she gives a small nod, probably to make her feel braver, and repeats them. "I want out. I did what you said. I let you keep those things in my house, ran your errands for you, let you—"

"Care to remind me *why* you were so willing to do those things?"

She frowns, picking at her fingernails. Good thing she has a mani-pedi scheduled. Eve likes to look her best, and that's hard to do when you pick at your nail polish like she does.

"I know what you did," she says, her voice still low. "But that doesn't mean I need to owe you for the rest of my life."

"Doesn't it?" I can't help the laugh that bubbles out of me. "My darling Eve, what are you going to do to stop me? Do you seriously think the police would let you get the first half of your story out before locking you up and throwing away the key?"

She shifts her weight in the seat, looking uncomfortable, and then glances around the restaurant. "I thought we could come to an agreement."

"We did." I plant one hand on the table to get her attention. "We did come to an agreement, or did you forget? I scratched your back; now you scratch mine."

"But it was supposed to be a one-time thing!" Her voice is too loud, and in recognition of that, she closes her eyes and takes a few deep breaths. "You blackmailed me. How is that *you* scratching my back? I don't see why I have to keep helping you out every time you call. It isn't fair."

"Fair." It's not a word I use often because I don't believe in things being fair. I believe in working hard to get the things you want, and that's what I've done my entire life. "You don't think us keeping quiet about what you did is worth you owing me a few favors from time to time? If you don't think that staying out of prison is far better than being sent to it, then I'm sure I can have that arranged."

She shakes her head, her silky, blonde hair spilling around her face. When she pushes it back, she sighs and bites her lower lip. It's a practiced move, and one I'm sure would work on a man who was interested in her.

"You don't get it," she says.

"Oh, I get it. I get that you needed my help and came crying to me. And now you want to what... walk away from our agreement?"

"No. I want to change it. I don't want those things in my house. I don't want to be your little errand girl. It's not safe."

I watch her, trying to decide how far Eve's willing to push this. She was willing to put her twin sister in prison so she could murder her own husband and get his money. Now, a few years into what's been an incredible relationship for both of us, she's not sure she wants to play the game any longer.

"Fine." I clear my throat, pushing back from the table. "I hope your garage is big enough to hold more than any expensive toys you might be collecting."

"What do you mean?" She stands up too, her fingertips resting on the table as she stares at me. "What kind of a threat is that?"

"Not a threat. It sounds like I need to bring by something

bigger so you can hang onto it for a little while—just so you can show me you're willing to play by *my* rules."

"You can't do this."

"I can. I own you, Eve, in case you've forgotten."

"She's out of prison." The words fly out of her mouth. "Don't you think we should talk about this? Don't you think we should figure out what we're going to do?"

I stare at her, trying to conjure up some emotion for her other than frustration, but that is all she warrants right now.

"What are you worried about, Eve? Your alibi is airtight. The police had no reason to suspect you of murder, and they still don't. You can't honestly think they'll come back to you now. Why in the world would they waste their time with you?"

She doesn't answer. A waitress walks by with a tray of food on her hand, but it's almost like Eve and I are invisible. Nobody looks at us; nobody speaks to us. The world moves on around us, but we are standing still.

Then it hits me. "You're afraid of her. You think what... that she's going to come for you?"

She simply stares at me, her eyes wide. I hit the nail on the head, I know it.

"You really think that you will be her first visit?"

"She already came by. What if she hurts me, what will you do then?"

I see it in Eve's eyes—she thinks this is her trump card, how she'll get me to play by her rules, but that's not how I play the game.

"She won't hurt you." I'm confident she won't.

Her shoulders slump a little bit as my words wash over her.

I continue, "You're smart, Eve. Keep her at bay. She's been in prison for years, and you have your perfect little life to fight for. Don't lose it."

7

MILLIE

TUESDAY

It takes more than a week for me to get my new ID in the mail, and I'm almost out of money by the time the slim envelope is delivered to the front office of the hotel I call home. Every day I go for a run. Every day I try to push down the hope that all of my belongings are still locked in a storage building. Even if Eve saved them, only she knows where they are.

I could ask her, but she wouldn't tell me.

Even if she did, I don't want my stuff anymore. My old clothes belong to Millie, a sad woman who didn't know her twin had it out for her.

They belong to the past me who didn't believe that anyone could hurt someone they loved as much as Eve hurt me. I've changed a lot since I last wore those clothes, and I don't want any of them back.

I have my sights set on much better things now.

I brush my hair, now as blonde as my sister's, and put on a pair of oversized sunglasses before checking my reflection in the bathroom mirror. They're from the dollar store a few blocks over, but hopefully nobody will notice that they're not name brand. I just have to keep moving, and nobody will get a good enough look at them.

"You've got this, Millie," I whisper to myself, double-checking that I look put together enough. There's a huge crack running down the side of the mirror. I avert my gaze from it, keep it focused on my reflection. Soon, I won't ever have to look in a cracked mirror again.

I'm sure that nothing in Eve's house is broken. It's all beautiful, new, designed to be the best. When I close my eyes for a moment, I can picture the layout of her house, and now that Joe is dead and she has the insurance payout from his death, I can only imagine how much nicer everything in the house is.

"But you won't have to imagine for long," I tell myself, grabbing my purse from the bed.

I still have to walk everywhere, and my feet in these heels will be killing me by the time I get to the bank, but at least I'll have access to my money.

It's not a lot, but it doesn't need to be. Just enough to get me through until I can access Eve's money.

I arrive at the bank. The teller behind the counter glances up at me as I walk up to her station. Her mouth drops open slightly when I push my ID across the counter to her. I look great in the new picture, a dead ringer for my sister. I sweep my sunglasses back with a smile.

"I'm back to access my account," I say, making sure my voice is loud enough for anyone who might want to listen in. "I know there were some problems with it being frozen before because I had been out of town, but hopefully everything is in order now."

She picks up the card and glances at the picture before giving me a curt nod. "Absolutely. I'm so sorry about that problem earlier. I'm sure you understand that we have to take care of our clients' accounts, and it was a little strange that yours was frozen by the government."

"I understand." Leaning forward, I drop my voice so she's the only one who gets to hear what I'm about to say next. "I want to withdraw everything from that account, but first I need you to give me a balance."

I'm not expecting much. Our parents always told me and Eve to look out for each other, but that was before they both died when we were in our twenties. The car accident should have been enough to bring us closer, but their death drove a wedge between us. Still, things didn't get bad for a while.

I was Eve's power of attorney before she got married and swapped me out for Joe, but I never once thought that having *her* as my power of attorney would be a mistake. We made that arrangement long before Eve killed her husband and placed the blame squarely on my shoulders. So nobody batted an eye when she waltzed into the bank, drained my account to pay for my lawyer, and then got rid of everything in my house right before the bank took it in repayment for my defaulted loan.

I'm not sure how much money is in the account now, but I need it all. I have to do a little more planning to make sure that when I take my sister down, there aren't any problems.

"Looks like you have two thousand, three hundred and fifty-seven dollars." The woman raises an eyebrow as she waits for me to respond. "And twenty-nine cents, of course. Would you like that in a cashier's check?"

"Cash," I tell her. I have no plans to set up a new account anywhere else in my name, and my debit card is expired. I can only imagine how long it would take to order a new one and have it sent to me. No, it's better I collect all the money and get out of here.

"Just a moment." The teller writes the amount on a slip of paper, then passes it to me to sign, before opening her drawer and counting out all the money I have in the world. A moment later, she's tucked it neatly into an envelope and slides it across the counter to me. "Is there anything else you need today?"

"This is it, thanks."

I flash her a big smile and grab my envelope, stuffing it into my purse as I walk out of the bank. As much as I'd love to go shopping and treat myself to a new purse or fresh lipstick, I'm on a tight schedule and an even tighter budget.

I know exactly where Eve is going to be, and I need to be there to watch her. She has no idea I've been following her, no idea I'm coming for her. Every single time I see her, she has her phone pressed up against her ear. For someone with enough money to buy whatever she wants, I'm surprised she doesn't have a personal assistant to handle her calls.

That's fine. Maybe I will get a PA when I become her. Or maybe I'll tell the people who keep calling her that I'm not interested in dealing with them any longer.

Outside the bank, I walk a few blocks over, grateful that we live in such a small town. I hated the place growing up, hated how everyone knew everything about you, but now I appreciate that I can get around without too much hassle.

Sure, the town has grown up some, and there are more people here than there were when we were younger, but it still has that small-town feel.

"Eve!"

I'm halfway across the street when I hear someone call my sister's name. I freeze, unsure if I should turn around and respond to the person, or check if they saw my twin.

"Eve, where are you going?"

Hearing no response from anyone else, I turn, grateful there aren't any people around to see me, and plaster a smile on my face. A tall, willowy woman wearing too much rouge on her cheeks and with long, brunette hair that billows behind her like a scarf runs up to me.

"I thought for a moment you didn't hear me. Where in the world are you running off to?"

Her words are friendly, but I hear some frustration in her tone—probably because I didn't immediately turn and acknowledge her. Maybe this is who Eve talks to on the phone all the time.

"Hey," I say, my heart slamming in my chest.

This is my first time pretending to be my sister. Fear eats at my confidence. I have no idea who this woman is— although I did see Eve having lunch with her yesterday. She has a gentle smile on her face that actually makes me relax.

I continue, "I'm headed to Pilates. Sorry I didn't hear you, I was thinking about that meal yesterday."

"Oh, God," she groans, grinning at me and slipping her arm through mine. "Wasn't it amazing? There's something about eating pasta in the middle of the day that makes it feel illegal." She laughs. "But you'd know about that, wouldn't you?"

When I look at her, I'm surprised to see her expression is tight, her eyes locked on mine.

"Tell me about it." I smile back at the woman on my arm, trying to rid myself of the uncomfortable feeling in the pit of my stomach. She's friendly, all smiles, and as I look at her, I take in her stylish earrings, smell the delicious perfume she wears, watch how her eyes dart even when we've reached the safety of the sidewalk. "I've always loved pasta."

"Same time next week, then? You know I love catching up with you to make sure everything's going smoothly." The woman faces me. She grips my shoulders tight; her fingers dig into my flesh a little bit. It's uncomfortable, but I don't try to pull away. "I know you have to run to Pilates—even though you already look amazing—and I wish we could talk more, but I've got to get to my next appointment before I'm late. And you have that little errand to run. See you Thursday for nails?"

"Definitely. Remind me what time?" I'm hoping she and Eve don't have a standing appointment when I ask the question, but I have to know where to find my sister the day after tomorrow.

The woman narrows her eyes at my question. "Is that a joke? Two o'clock, the same as every other Thursday. Are you feeling okay?"

I don't know why her question sits wrong with me, but I pull away from her, my heart beating faster.

It wasn't a threat. No way was that question a threat, but there was definitely something off about the way she asked me that makes my skin crawl.

"I think I need a nap. I'm simply exhausted," I say, holding my breath and hoping my excuse will work.

"Maybe you should get one so you can get your head on straight," she says, tilting her own. Then she spins away from me and hurries down the sidewalk.

I really want to celebrate, to be pleased that my first encounter as Eve fooled the woman, but something wasn't right with our interaction.

"You're paranoid and used to everything blowing up in your face," I tell myself, in an effort to pep myself back up.

I walk over to a bench in front of the restaurant, muttering.

"I just have to watch Eve a little longer, and then I'll finally be able to become her."

I ignore the fact that I have no idea what errand the woman was talking about. It doesn't matter, though, does it? Eve knows, and she'll take care of the errand. I only need a bit longer to figure everything out.

I sit down, making sure I'm in the shade so nobody walking by can easily see my face, then cross one leg over the other and wait for Eve to show up. She should be here soon. Three times a week she has Pilates, and now I know at 2 pm on Thursday she has her weekly nail appointment. I pull a notepad from my purse, flip to the page where I'm writing out her schedule and make a note of it.

I pause, then write *errand?* on the next line. Eve's a busy woman, that's for sure. I don't get the feeling she's involved with any charity group, but something or somebody has her running all over town.

Without a car, I have no easy way to follow her so I can see what she's up to.

I wish I caught the name of the woman she's going to the salon with, but there wasn't any way I could ask without sounding even more suspicious.

I'm tapping my pen against the notepad, thinking about how to find out her name, when movement down the sidewalk makes me glance up. It's the woman I just talked to. Her hands are flapping angrily in the air while she talks.

What in the world is going on?

Her back is to me, and I can't see whom she's talking to, so I shift on the bench, angling my body to get a better view.

But I don't have to angle myself to see anything, because at that moment, the woman turns and points, and I watch with dread as my twin stalks angrily toward me.

8

MILLIE

TUESDAY

"What the hell do you think you're doing?" Eve hisses the words at me. She's standing over me, her body tight with emotion, her hands clenched into fists at her sides. "Why were you talking to Mya, pretending to be me?"

Mya. Got it.

"I was just being friendly," I say, standing up so my sister can't continue to tower over me. "She approached me and thought I was you."

"It didn't cross your mind to let her know she had the wrong person?"

I shake my head, some of the confidence I had earlier draining out of me. "She started talking, and before I knew what happened, she was walking away. I didn't do anything, Eve. You need more observant friends."

Her mouth drops open. "I don't know what you're doing

here, Millie, but you're not welcome here. You murdered my husband."

"Oh, my God," I say, throwing my hands up in the air. "You're back on that? You know full well, Eve, that you're the one who killed Joe and blamed it on me. I came by your house the day I got out of prison to let you know I forgive you."

Am I totally sure she killed Joe? No, not one hundred percent, but it's the only thing that makes any sense, and I'm going with it.

I see the rage that flashes across her face at my accusation, and her eyes narrow.

"Forgive me?" She inhales hard, her cheeks hollowing, then exhales. "You're insane, you know that? Insane. I don't know what this is—" she waves a hand over my body and hair "—but I'm not a good look on you. You look ridiculous trying to be me."

"I'm not trying to be you." I grit my teeth, and I'm suddenly having trouble breathing. "I'm just trying to get my life back. The one you stole from me, remember? Tell me, dear sister, when the bank took my house and you cleaned it out, did you at least put my things in storage?"

I know the answer to the question, and there's a voice in my head telling me that I don't want to ask this, but the words are out of my mouth before I can stop them.

A slow smile spreads across her face, showing off her blindingly white teeth.

I need to get my teeth whitened.

"I sent it to the dump." She pops the *P*, clearly enjoying driving home the fact that everything I owned is gone. "All of it. It was junk, and I didn't think even a charity shop would want to take it."

"You're evil," I tell her. I feel heat creeping up the back of my neck. I have to take a deep breath to keep from screaming at her. "Why would you do this to me?"

"I cleaned up your mess." She bats her eyes at me, doing her best to look innocent "Now, if you'll excuse me, Millie, I have Pilates to get to. If you continue to follow me and harass my friends, I'd love to call the cops." She taps her chin. "You think we'd be lucky enough to get the same officer who arrested you before?"

I don't answer.

"Go away, Millie. I don't want you here. You're not welcome." With that, she spins away from me, and her heels click on the pavement as she walks up to the Pilates building.

I watch her as she enters, watch as the door closes behind her. My original plan was to sit here and watch where she went after her class, but when I turn and look down the sidewalk, her friend is standing there, watching me.

Mya.

I smile at her.

She may be Eve's friend now, but she won't be for long.

Soon, she'll be mine.

9

EVE

TUESDAY

"I'm supposed to meet someone named Rusty," I mutter to myself, looking down at my cell phone. "Who the hell would name their kid that?"

My breath catches in my throat as I turn the corner in the abandoned factory and see an empty parking lot, a line of trees beyond that, and an overflowing trash can. Of all the places Gareth has sent me, this has got to be one of the worst. I know he's not exactly concerned with my safety, but I can't help wishing he would be a bit more selective about where he sends me to complete his drops.

I'm sure that when this place was in business, it was hopping, with people coming and going all day long. But I haven't seen another person since I turned down the side road that winds next to the river before ending in this parking lot. I shield my eyes from the sun and glance around, waiting for Rusty to arrive.

It's still early afternoon, and the bright sun burns my shoulders and back. I try to ignore the beads of sweat running between my shoulder blades. This is worse than hot yoga. Worse than that time I pretended to be a runner so I could meet cute guys, and ended up sucked into a half-marathon on Thanksgiving. Worse than—

"Eve?"

The man's voice coming from behind startles me, and I jump, causing me to whip around and glare at him. He snuck up on me a lot easier than I expected. I shiver when my imagination at being alone with him starts to run away from me.

"Yeah, I'm Eve." My bag cuts into my shoulder. I shift it so it doesn't hurt as much. "You're Rusty?"

It's a silly question to ask. There's no way anyone else would be looking for me out here in the middle of nowhere, or know enough to call me by my first name, but I'm nothing if not thorough. The fear of what Gareth would do to me if I make a mistake is enough to keep me vigilant.

The man laughs. He wears ripped jeans and a dark T-shirt. Unlike me, who's sweating profusely, he seems relaxed and comfortable standing in the hot sun. His nose is too big for his face, and he wears one large gold ring on each hand. I tear my eyes away from the glint of the sun on the rings and look up at his face.

"Do you have the money?" I ask.

The first time Gareth told me I was going to be working for him, I said I was afraid, that there was nothing to stop those I met from hurting me. But he laughed.

They know you belong to me, he said—like that was going to make me feel any better.

"I have it right here. You want to count it out?" The man pulls out a thick wad of cash from his pocket. I nod. I stay put, because I don't want to get any closer to him than I have to.

But when he reaches the money out, he keeps his hand far enough back that I'm going to have to step in closer to take it.

With a hard inhale I do that, exhaling when my hand closes on the money.

He doesn't let it go right away. Instead he tugs it and me closer to him, a grin on his face.

"Maybe later we could get a drink," he says.

"Never mix business with pleasure," I chide him, freeing the cash from his hand.

I feel exposed having to step back from him to count it, but I do and flick through the bills quickly. The first time I did this it took me so long to count the money, the buyer got uncomfortable and threatened to leave. But now I move faster than before, and when I'm done, I nod once, pocketing the cash into my bag that I drop down from my shoulder.

The pills I'm supposed to give him are in bottles, wrapped in a tight little package. They rattle some when I hand them over, but that's hardly my problem. I don't know where Rusty is going to sell them, whom he's going to give them to— anything. I don't want to know. My part in this is almost over, and I can't wait to get out of here.

"You're more than welcome to open it up and check them," I say, wiping my hand on my jeans, like I'm going to rid myself of the feeling of my skin crawling. "But you know Gareth, and you should know that he wouldn't ever sell anyone short."

"I'm not worried about that, Eve." Rusty grins at me.

I take an involuntary step back. How many times have I made these drops for Gareth? You'd think by now that I'd be an expert and that nothing could throw me for a loop, but I can't help the fact that I don't like being near this guy. Nobody who sells drugs is going to be a stand-up person, but there's something about Rusty that makes me feel dirty.

The bag on my shoulder is as heavy as before, stuffed with money now and not pills.

"Well, have a good day."

I turn away from Rusty before he has a chance to respond. I just want to get the hell out of here in one piece. As I walk away, I keep thinking I hear footsteps following behind me all the way to the parking lot, but when I get in my car and lock the door, I see that Rusty has already disappeared.

"Probably crawled back under whatever rock he was under before," I mutter to myself, cranking the engine and turning the AC as high as it will go. "I don't know where Gareth finds these creeps."

I know I need to call Gareth and let him know the drop is complete, but right now I just want to get out of this parking lot and back into town. It's one thing to come here for a deal but another to sit here in the parking lot completely exposed. Driving quickly, I keep my eyes peeled for Rusty so I can be sure he isn't going to follow me out of here, but there's no sign of the drug dealer.

At the first red light I come to, I dial Gareth's number, wincing a little when the sound of his deep voice fills the car.

"Eve, my favorite little task rabbit. How did it go with Rusty?" He sounds happy. I get the feeling he was laughing with someone right before I called. My stomach tightens at the thought of whom he might spend his time with.

"It was fine. I have the money." The light flips to green, and I turn the car to the right, glancing once more in my rearview mirror as I do.

No Rusty.

"Great. Take it to your house and make sure you lock the doors up nice and tight."

I nod, then remember he can't see me. I grip the steering wheel so hard that my hands start to cramp. With a deep exhale, I focus on relaxing my grip. "Okay. I'll do that. Thanks, Gareth."

"Oh, no, thank you, Eve. You're so helpful. I'll be by in a bit to get the money, so don't get any funny ideas about spending it."

Someone near him laughs; the sound is bright and weightless. I recognize it.

Mya.

Of course she'd be with him right now. They're the only two who can stand each other. I grimace, then tap the red button on my screen to end the call.

I feel dizzy, just like I did the first time I completed a sale for Gareth. He told me it was no big deal, that anyone could do it, but I still felt sick to my stomach. Each drop was supposed to get easier, or that was what I told myself, but they never seem to.

It doesn't matter if I'm meeting someone in a park downtown or an abandoned parking lot, I still feel like someone is going to arrest me and haul me away.

"You need to get your head on straight," I say, breaking the heavy silence in the car. "You got one person killed before, so why not another? Then you know what you could do, Eve? You could live your life."

The idea eats at me. Why not kill Gareth like I killed Joe? Why not make sure he can't ever bother me again?

Sure, there are more moving parts. There's Mya; there's the men he works with.

I tighten my grip on the steering wheel again. Desperation washes over me when I think about how to get out from under his thumb.

There's my sister.

I zip past the yoga studio where I spend much of my time, and punch the gas when I get closer to the house.

I might talk a big game about hurting Gareth or Millie so

I might get out of this situation, but I know I won't. As much as I'd like to think I have a way out of this, I'm pretty sure I only have two options.

Go to prison like my sister.

Or die.

And I'm not terribly keen on doing either.

"Tomorrow's Wednesday," I remind myself as I pull into my driveway and mash the button to raise the garage door. "Wednesday nights are for you, Eve, and nobody can take them from you."

I pull the car in, mash another button to drop the door behind me, and sit in the dark for a few minutes.

Even though I know the chances of me killing Gareth and walking away from it in one piece are slim to none, I can't get the thought out of my head. I imagine him like Joe—dead and unable to bother me ever again.

It would be so sweet.

Nobody can stop me dreaming, right? Just like nobody can stop me worrying about what Millie has planned, or thinking about how to stop her from ruining my life.

In the end, it's going to be them or me, and I don't want it to be me.

10

MILLIE

WEDNESDAY

My sister leaves the house, backing her expensive black car down the driveway, looking over her shoulder for anything that might be in her path.

I stand off to the side, watching from the woods. I'm silent, waiting. My feet hurt from standing here all day, but I know from watching her last week that she went somewhere on Wednesday evenings.

I don't know where, and there's no good way to find out without getting into her house.

As soon as her car is out of the driveway and she's driving down the road, I step out from my spot behind the tree. My hands hurt a little bit from where the bark cut into the skin. I rub them on my jeans as I walk up to her front porch.

I don't see any security cameras, but that doesn't mean she doesn't have them. Still, when I don't spot any red eyes winking at me, I walk up to the door, stand on my tiptoes, and feel around the top frame for a key.

Nothing.

"Where did you put it?" I ask, stepping back and looking under the mat. "Everyone has a spare they hide somewhere, so where the hell is yours?"

I don't see any fake rocks in the garden, but I still backtrack down the front walk to the driveway, my head on a swivel as I look for an obvious hiding place for her key.

"You okay over there?" A deep voice pulls me from my search. I look up and stare at the house across the street. A tall man in khaki pants wearing a tie tied too tightly around his neck is standing at his mailbox, a stack of letters in his hand.

"I've lost my key," I say, shrugging, pretending it's no big deal. "Can you believe that? Locked out. I don't want to call a locksmith." While I speak, I walk down the driveway toward him. "Don't worry about me though. I'll figure it out."

The last thing I want is for a neighbor to get involved and then say something to Eve later about helping her out.

"Hang on one second, I'll grab you the spare." The man holds up one finger and then hurries up to his house.

I'm nervous. Getting someone else involved—anyone else involved—isn't the plan, but I need that key.

A moment later the man comes back out, waving the key above his head. He still has his mail in his other hand, and I glance at the name on one envelope when he walks up to me.

"You're the best, Mitch," I say, praying that the name on the letter is the right one. "Seriously, a lifesaver."

"Don't you worry one bit, Eve. I get concerned about you in this big house by yourself, so I'm glad you gave Sara a key. Just bring it back over if you'd like us to keep it for you, but there's no rush."

"You two are the best." I grin at him and rack my brain for

something else to say. "You know, whatever you're doing to your grass is working."

"You think so?" He visibly swells with pride. "Yeah, I told Sara we needed to do something to compete with your fabulous yard. Whenever you're finally willing to reveal the name of your landscaper, let us know!"

"Maybe one of these days," I call over my shoulder as I walk up to the house. Once on the porch, I check my watch. I gave myself an hour to handle everything, and I have only fifty minutes left.

Exhaling hard, I put the key in the lock and turn it, praying that the door will open.

It does.

An antiseptic smell hits my nose immediately and causes it to wrinkle. I shake my head to try to clear the smell. It's harsh and irritating, and I wonder what my sister needed to clean that she required chemicals. She's always been something of a neat freak, but this is taking it a little too far. I remember my mom saying Eve cleaned whenever she was nervous, but what in her amazing life could put her so on edge?

"Okay, darling Eve, what are you hiding in here?"

I close the door behind me and lock it, slipping the key into my pocket. Even though it's been years since I was in this house, most of it still looks the same. She hasn't changed the main furniture in the living room, and I walk in there first, kicking my shoes off so I don't accidentally leave any dirty footprints behind.

The kitchen is the same, too. I look for a planner on the counter, but I don't see one. My stomach growls as I walk by her fridge. I stop and take a peek inside, not surprised to see it filled with organic produce and several Buddha bowls from a restaurant I don't recognize.

"I can't wait to get in here," I say, trailing my fingers across the quartz countertops. "This place is amazing."

Eve has managed to create the dream life for herself, and I hate her for it. I walk through the living room and past a music room, where a baby grand piano sits, sheet music at the ready, and reach the staircase.

"There has to be something up here," I say to myself, grabbing the railing and taking the first step. I'm nervous, not because I think she's going to come home and find me, but because I might not find what I need up here.

I need to know everything about my sister before I can take over her life.

If she has any secrets, any at all, then this won't work.

I'm halfway up the stairs when the doorbell rings.

11

MILLIE

WEDNESDAY

I open the door and see the last person I expected.

Surprise flickers across her face, but she smirks, quickly covering whatever emotion she was experiencing.

"Good, you're here." Mya's current mood is difficult for me to read.

I grip the door in shock, staring at her while I try to figure out what she's doing here.

"I never did understand why Gareth let you have Wednesday nights off. But you're here." She chuckles. "Does this mean that you finally decided to help us out on Wednesdays the way I said you should?"

She clutches a bottle of wine in her hand, her grip tight around the neck so she doesn't drop it. As she speaks, she tilts her head slightly, like she's trying to anticipate what I'm going to say next.

"Not yet," I say, leaning against the doorframe the same way I saw Eve do the day I showed up at her house. "But my plans changed for the evening." As I glance down at my watch, to make a show of how strange my evening has become, I feel my stomach twist.

My time is running out. The real Eve will be home soon, and I still don't have enough information on her to feel confident I can pretend to be her. If I killed her now, I wouldn't know exactly how to act like her, to take over her life. The last thing I need is for her to come home and find me in her house.

The thought is both terrifying and exhilarating. If I could get Mya to leave so I could handle Eve on my own, then I might be able to take care of things tonight. But I'm not quite ready for that phase of the plan.

"Hmm," she says, brushing past me to enter the house. "I was hoping you were going to say that you had cancelled your Wednesday nights. Having you wrapped up every single week makes it difficult for us to work around your schedule sometimes, you know."

I don't answer. Really, what is there for me to say?

Ignoring me, she walks into the kitchen and sighs before reaching out and flicking on a light. "You have it so dark in here, Eve. Lord."

I follow her, doing my best to keep from looking as nervous as I feel. I have no idea why this woman is in Eve's house or what she wants. I never should have let her in, and now I have to worry about how to get her to leave. How I'm going to manage that without her wondering what's going on with me. Well, I'm not entirely sure what *is* going on.

"What's the wine for?" I ask casually, pulling out a stool and sitting down at the counter, pretending it's something I do every night. "Did I miss a special occasion?"

For a moment, I'm not sure she's going to answer. She puts the bottle of wine down on the counter with a *thunk*, then slides it toward me.

"I thought we could have a drink since you're home. To make sure we're still on the same page. Besides, how can I make sure you're not going to do something stupid unless I check in with you from time to time?"

When I don't answer her, she grins at me. There's something creepy about her smile, about the way it doesn't reach her eyes, about the way she shows off too many teeth, that makes a shiver dance its way up my spine.

"You don't have much to say, do you?" Mya says. "Don't you want to have a drink with me and make sure we're on the same page about everything?"

I have no idea what this woman is talking about, but the last thing I want to do is have a glass of wine with her. I haven't had alcohol for a long time. I can only imagine how chatty I might get, what secrets I might spill, once I have some vino and my tongue unsticks from the roof of my mouth.

Not to mention that wherever Eve is this evening, I can't expect that she'll stay there much longer.

"Tonight's not good," I tell her, putting what I hope looks like a real smile on my face. "I appreciate you coming by, Mya, it means a lot, but I'm headed up to bed. I feel pretty sick, actually, and drinking would probably only exacerbate it." I stifle a yawn, hoping it will be enough to sell my lie.

Mya tilts her head as she stares at me, her expression tight.

"Why are you so tired? You never go to bed this early." Her voice is sharp. Accusatory. "There isn't something making you regret working with us, is there?"

I stare at her. There's no good lie coming to my tongue.

Heat starts to creep up the back of my neck, and I wish more than anything that I had never opened the door.

"It's Millie, isn't it?"

My name on her lips makes me freeze in place.

Does she know who I am?

Fear eats away at me that my cover is blown. But I pause a moment when I realize she's waiting for a response. It hits me then that she thinks Millie is the problem, not that *I'm* Millie.

Slowly, I nod. Mya's staring at me like she's never seen me before in her life, and I know I need to get her out of the house. The best thing I can think of is to channel my sister.

"You got it." I flip my hair over my shoulder, a habit I've seen Eve do a dozen times since watching her, then plaster a scowl on my face. "She thinks she can walk back into my life after killing Joe, and I'm going to open my arms to her? Yeah, right."

Something I say catches Mya off guard, but she quickly recovers.

"But she's out of jail," she says, an edge to her voice. "So they obviously don't think she killed him. Your alibi will hold, but what are you going to do?"

What am I going to do about what, Mya?

I shrug, doing my best to look casual. "Nothing. There's nothing to do."

"She's going to be a problem."

Was that a question or a statement?

"Maybe. I don't think so. I have a good feeling she'll be leaving town soon when she realizes there isn't anything here for her." I glance down at the bottle of wine on the counter as if I just remembered it's there. "Listen, I appreciate you coming by, but I need to get to bed."

"We want to know what you're going to do about your sister." Mya pushes back from the counter. "You need to have a plan, Eve. It's not every day that the woman you sent to jail for your husband's murder gets out and comes looking for you."

There it is. She knows Eve framed me for Joe's death.

I can't breathe. The air in this kitchen is suddenly too tight, too heavy. It presses down on my chest. I open my mouth to say something, but nothing comes out. So I nod, unsure of what else to do.

"The last thing you want is to get caught up in something with her," she tells me, shrugging. "You know as well as I do how that could end, and I'm sure you don't want it to turn ugly."

"I'm careful." I'm not sure what to say to Mya, but I obviously have to say something.

"You'd better be."

Immediately, all the tension in the room ticks up a degree. The air feels tighter and hotter, and I swallow hard, hoping that I can convince her nothing bad is going on.

She pauses, still watching me too closely. Her suspicious gaze flicks across my face, and then she finally smiles, making me relax. I don't know what that interrogation was, but things seem better between us now. Settled.

"Right." Mya taps the bottle of wine with her finger. "Since you obviously have a lot going on tonight, and we already agreed that Wednesday was your night off, why don't you bring this tomorrow when we get our nails done? It's good stuff, and I don't want you drinking it without me."

There it is again—her disarming grin that throws me for a loop. She doesn't look like she's angry with me, doesn't look like she knows who I am, but for a moment there...

You know what? No.

I close my eyes for a moment and focus on where I am. I'm in Eve's kitchen—soon to be my new kitchen. I'm no longer in prison, no longer worried about what other people might do to me when I turn my back.

Mya is intense, that's for sure, but that doesn't mean she's a bad person. It means she comes across a little hard sometimes. I can handle that. I lived with that.

But if she knows everything, then I have to be careful. Did Eve open up to her? Did Eve get too drunk one night and spill everything to this woman about how she ruined my life?

And if Mya knows the truth, why wouldn't she do something about it? The thought that someone on the outside knew what my sister did to me and didn't try to help makes me sick.

I have no idea how Mya knows the truth, but it scares me that she does. Right now, though, I don't want to think about her, not when I still have to deal with Eve.

Not when I haven't finished taking over my sister's life yet.

"I'll bring it," I tell her, finally opening my eyes and smiling at her again. "Really, Mya, you didn't have to do this, but it means a lot to me that you would come by."

"Well, you mean a lot to us. You know that." Her smile looks kind, but I'm not convinced it reaches her eyes. Something stirs in my stomach, a worry, but I push it away.

"Same." It's time to lay on the charm, if only to get her out of the house so I can decide what to do about my twin. Mya's intense. It makes sense to me that Eve would find an intense woman to be friends with. It doesn't mean anything else, doesn't mean that she's on to me.

She eyes me. "Don't let her ruin everything, Eve." When I don't answer, she sashays out of the kitchen, letting herself out of the house without another word.

I rush to the front door and close it behind her with a hard exhale. I lean against it even after I lock it. It feels strange to engage so many locks, but Eve has them for a reason. I'm not going to be here much longer tonight, and she has her door locked this way for a reason.

I don't know what she's scared of, and I'm not interested in finding out.

"How in the world am I supposed to get Eve to bring that wine to the nail appointment with Mya tomorrow?" I whisper the question to myself, still leaning against the door. My mind races as I try to work out the problem, but I don't have a solution.

Fear prickles the back of my neck, and I hurry back to the kitchen to look at the bottle of wine.

"Blood Sisters Winery," I whisper, frowning at it as I sink down onto a stool.

I'm unsure of what to do next.

"I can't let Eve know I was in her house," I say, standing back up and pacing back and forth. "I can't let Mya know she was talking to me and not Eve. Coming here was a mistake." I press my fingers hard into my temples as I try to work out what to do next.

It feels like there are rubber bands wrapped too tight around my chest, and I'm having trouble breathing.

"You have to calm down, Millie," I tell myself, smacking my hand on the counter. "You have to get a grip. Eve will be home soon, and you'd better figure out what you're going to do with this bottle of wine before that happens."

I wanted another week at least to figure out how I was going to handle Eve. I wanted more time to get prepared, to make sure I knew what I was doing before I became her. But now I don't think I have that time.

The wine calls to me, and I feel my mouth water, but instead of opening the bottle, I walk out of the kitchen to the garage.

I don't have a lot of time to get ready before Eve comes home.

I'm going to have to move my timeline up if I'm to get what I want, but I'll still come out on top. I want Eve's perfect life. I want her Pilates classes, her nail dates, her lunches with friends.

I want her expensive clothes, her bouncy hair, her freedom as she waltzes through life without any problems. She was out here, free, living her best life while I was in hell.

It's my turn.

12

EVE

WEDNESDAY

My fingers drum a staccato beat on the steering wheel as I drive across town to my house. I'm not in a rush to get home, not looking forward to being in the quiet house by myself, staring out the window every time I hear a car drive by.

I want out of there. Sure, my life looks perfect on the outside. It was, once. For a few years, at least.

Until I met them.

A shiver crawls up my spine when I think about the first time they showed up at my house. I was happy on the inside that Joe was gone, while still playing the role of the grieving widow on the outside.

And then my life fell apart.

With a shaking of my head, I try to clear the memories. It's almost impossible. Wednesday night is my one time a week when I can get out of the house and live my life on my terms. I know it's dangerous, and there's a very good chance it won't end well for me, but I have to do it.

I have to feel something in my life other than fear.

When I hired the hitman to kill Joe, I did it because I needed out. I couldn't live married to a man I'd grown to resent any longer. All I wanted was to have the life he promised me when I walked down that aisle. How in the world was I supposed to know the man I married would much rather hoard his money than spend it on anything for me?

I couldn't do it. The man was loaded, with more insurance policies on his life than anyone needs. I always thought it was a little silly for him to have so much and spend it on nothing. That was before I realized I could get that insurance money for myself and came up with my plan. As soon as it dawned on me that I could live the life I always wanted—without Joe —I knew I had to do it.

Honestly, though, I never thought it would come to this. I'm a grown woman with plenty of money to my name, but I'm sneaking around, doing what others tell me to, because I don't have a choice in the matter.

There's a sad song on the radio. I turn the knob hard to the left, shutting it off. I'm annoyed as I drive, not just at the singer, but at myself, for letting things get this far.

A soft beep from my phone breaks the silence in the car before the ringtone starts to play a melody. I swear and grab it from the cupholder, then swipe the screen while trying to keep my eyes on the road.

I hit the answer key.

"You know I'm busy on Wednesday nights," I say, gritting my teeth.

"Oh, Eve, is that any way to speak to your friend?" Gareth's voice is low, oily. It always makes me shiver to hear him speak, and right now is no different.

When I don't answer, he continues, "I have a big job for you this weekend, and you'll need to be in town."

I'll be here. Of course I'll be here. This courtesy call isn't because he wants to make sure I'm going to be around, but because he wants me to know he has this kind of power over me.

"You don't have any questions?" he says. "Don't you want to talk it over, to make sure you know exactly what you're going to have to do?"

I shake my head even though he can't see me. "No. You know I'll do it because it's not like I have a choice." There's venom in my words, and when he laughs, I hate him more.

"You don't have a choice. I know it. You know it. I like to make sure from time to time that you understand where you stand. Be good, Eve. I'll see you soon."

I want to throw up. I toss my phone into the passenger seat, then grip the steering wheel hard until my hands cramp. Just like that, my night is ruined.

Just like that, I'm reminded of the horror of what my life really is. I take a deep breath in through my nose and then exhale, trying to do everything in my power to keep from screaming.

It wasn't ever supposed to be like this.

When I pull into the garage at my house, I sit in my car for a few minutes, listening to the engine cool. It clicks quietly in the dark, and as it does, I feel my blood pressure come back down. As much as I'd like to do something to get out of my situation, I'm stuck for a little bit longer.

"Okay, let's fix tonight," I say, grabbing my phone and navigating to my messages. My finger hovers over the most recent ones I received. I don't want to delete them. I don't want to keep playing this game of keeping *him* hidden.

But my phone isn't really my phone, and if someone wants to check it, they will. I can't have them looking at these messages. It hurts me more than anything else in the world to press my finger on the number and hold it down until the little trashcan icon pops up.

I have to delete the messages we sent each other.

Nobody can look at my phone and discover whom I've been talking to.

At this point, it isn't just my life on the line.

13

MILLIE

WEDNESDAY

The sound of the garage door opening makes my stomach clench.

I have every light in the house turned off so Eve won't see me sitting here waiting on her, and I'm forcing myself to breathe slowly.

In through the mouth. Out through the nose. I'm the only person in the world who can control my own breathing, who can make sure that I make it through this in one piece. Closing my eyes, I try to stay as calm as possible when I hear Eve open the inner door inside the garage and step inside the house.

"The balls on that man," she mutters.

But I don't even care what she's talking about right now. What matters to me is ending this.

Becoming Eve.

"He thinks he can walk all over me. He thinks he has

complete control of the situation, but he doesn't know that I'm through playing his little games."

Whatever problem Eve is having with a man, I'm more than happy to take care of it.

When I'm Eve.

She stalks into the kitchen, her heels clicking loudly; then she kicks them off. I hear them clatter on the floor, hear her push them out of the way so she won't trip on them later.

"What I need is a drink!"

She screams the words, and I wince, surprised to hear that much emotion coming from her. Did she have that much emotion when she killed Joe and framed me for it? Did she feel that much emotion when she sobbed to the police that she couldn't believe I would do this to her?

I'm not sure, but I sure as hell want to find out.

Pushing out of my seat in the living room, I'm still gripping the knife I took from her butcher block. It's heavy but perfectly weighted, the blade professionally sharpened, and I have no doubt it will do what I need done.

"Eve." I whisper her name as I come up behind her.

She whirls around, her eyes wide.

"What the hell are you doing here?" She spits the words at me, anger etched around her eyes. "How did you get in? What did you hear?"

What did I hear? That's a weird thing for her to be worried about when I'm standing in front of her with a knife. I assess her, trying to decide which one of us is stronger.

This isn't how I wanted things to go. I wanted to be prepared, with plastic down to make cleanup easier. I wanted time to prepare what I was going to say to her, but Mya's visit made everything move too fast.

"You owe me," I say, taking a step closer to her. "You owe me for taking my life."

She laughs, the sound loud and shrill. "You killed Joe, Millie."

It's the same thing I've heard her say a hundred times since the night she framed me, but never before have I heard her voice waver, like she's not entirely sure of what she's saying.

"You killed him. You framed me." I have the knife out in front, and my hand doesn't waver. I'm ready for this, ready to take what she owes me. "You never once felt bad about it. I came here before to tell you I forgave you, but I don't anymore."

"Yeah?" She's doing her best to sound brave, but she has to be a little scared. There's no way she's not. "And what the hell are you doing here, then?"

"You owe me a life," I tell her, lunging at her.

She cries out, taking a quick step back and throwing her hand up in the air to stop me.

I've never cut anyone before, never gotten into a fight, not even in prison. The feeling of the blade cutting her makes my stomach twist.

"Shit! You've lost your mind! I'm calling the cops, Millie." She grabs her cut arm, blood seeps out from between her fingers, and she tries to move. I step in front of her to keep her from going around me.

"No, Eve, this stops now."

I'm breathing hard, sucking in more air than breathing out, and it's difficult for me to focus. My vision is a little fuzzy. I blink hard, trying to clear it.

I continue, "You did this to me. You pushed me into this. What did you think was going to happen? Did you think you could walk away from your lies? Continue to live your fairy-tale life? No. Not when you took everything from me. Everything!"

I scream the last word at her and rush forward, her knife still in my hand.

It slips easily into her stomach. She cries out, gasping and bending over, clutching at her midsection as I pull the knife out and stab again.

And again.

I hear the prison chaplain's voice in my head telling me that I need to forgive Eve. I hear him talking to me about the years of pain I felt, about how I'm going to forgive my sister, about what I was going to say to her.

I hear it all, yet I can't focus on any of it. I'm only able to focus on the movement of my hand as it plunges in and out of Eve, on the way her face, once a mirror image of mine, twists.

"Please—" She drops to her knees.

I can't catch my breath. It smells like iron in here; the bitter scent of her blood is almost overwhelming. I want to wipe my nose, to clear the scent from the air, but I don't do it.

"Please," I mock, crouching down in front of her. She's kneeling in blood; it's pooling around her on the tiles. I can't imagine how difficult it will be to get blood out of grout, but right now I don't care. "Please don't ruin my life. Don't make me suffer like this. Is that what you were going to say, Eve? Because that's what I said to you, do you remember? I asked you not to ruin my life. I *begged* you."

"I'm sorry." Her face is pale. Even though she's clutching her stomach in hopes that doing so will save her, she has to know it's almost over. She has to know she's not walking away from this. "I'm sorry, Millie."

"I forgave you. I thought we could find closure." I stand up before looking down at her. There's blood on my shoe, but I'll throw it away. It doesn't matter. Nothing matters.

My sister doesn't respond.

"Your life is mine now," I tell her, reaching down to lift her chin so she has to look at me. "Do you hear me? Your life is mine. This... perfect life you've built? I'm taking it, and there's nothing you can do about it."

Her mouth opens and closes.

"What's that?" I hear the cruel tone in my voice, but I don't even try to soften it. I don't care how evil I sound right now. I want her to know how badly she messed up. "Did you want to say something, Eve? Don't let me stop you. I'm sure it's worth hearing."

"You... don't..."

Her fingers press into her stomach as she tries to stop the bleeding. I see how scared she is of dying right in front of me, but I don't care.

"I don't what? Want to do this? Believe me, dear sister, I do."

She shakes her head. Just once. "No... it's not..."

"Not what? Not what I want to do? Not fair? Not mine? Well, guess what, Eve, you're wrong. It *is* mine. All of this, your home, your Pilates class, your clothes and food? It's mine. You took so many things from me—so many! And now you need to pay me back."

"Perfect." She breathes out the word.

I laugh. *Perfect.* It is. All of this. I don't think I could be happier.

"It is perfect," I say, grinning at her.

She falls forward, catching herself at the last minute, then flops to the floor.

"You're absolutely right, Eve."

It has to be perfect. This wasn't the plan, but it is now, and I don't see a single way this won't work out just the way I want.

14

MILLIE

WEDNESDAY

The only thing I want to do is take a hot shower.

I'm exhausted from dragging Eve's body out of the house and burying her in the woods. My hands are raw from gripping the shovel so hard. My knees ache from kneeling on the kitchen tile while I cleaned up her blood.

This wasn't how any of this was supposed to go.

That refrain runs through my head over and over until it becomes background noise, an earworm I can't get out. I didn't think I was going to kill Eve today, but she didn't give me a choice.

She came home before I could get out of the house. She told someone that she framed me, and that person didn't do anything to help me. This is on Eve. She brought this on herself by killing her husband and sending me to jail.

I keep telling myself that. I didn't have a choice. My sister took my right to choose from me and forced me to kill her.

Even in the shower, I feel dirty. It feels like Eve's blood is still coating my skin. I drag the loofah over my red skin again and again, scrubbing until it sloughs off the outer layer of skin. After, I'm feeling a little raw and exposed.

Multiple showerheads spray me from every direction, and I turn under them, letting them wash away the bubbles from the nicest body wash I've ever used. It smells like jasmine and vanilla, and while it's not the scent I would have chosen, I still feel like I'm at a spa.

I used the guest bathroom in case things got messy. So far, Eve's house looks clean, but I know I'm going to need to wash it really well.

Just not now.

Now I need to practice being Eve, and after I need to rest.

"Okay, Millie, you've got this," I say as I wrap a fluffy gray towel around myself and stand in front of the bathroom mirror. The floor is heated. I wiggle my toes on the bare tile.

Clearing my throat, I run my fingers through my blonde hair. It still feels strange, like I'm wearing someone else's hair. That thought makes me smile.

"Eve," I say, then shake my head. I can do this. Clearing my throat a second time, I look at my reflection. "I'm Eve." I plaster on a smile and hold out my hand, as if meeting someone for the first time. "It's simply lovely to meet you."

There. I can do this. I'll practice more. I'll make sure nobody will suspect that I'm not actually Eve. I have to be exactly like her, and I will be.

After leaving the guest bathroom, I wander down the hall, enjoying the feel of the wide, wooden planks under my bare feet. Everything about this house screams extravagance, and I can't help the soft sigh that leaves my lips when I turn on the bedroom light. She redecorated since Joe died, and it's more my style.

The large four-poster bed in the corner has a folded set of soft silk pajamas on the end of it. I drop my towel to the floor, where it pools around my feet, and slip them on. The pajamas are soft against my skin and fit like they were made for me. After, I walk over to her bedside table. I let out a little cry of delight when I see her planner sitting there.

"Thank goodness," I say, picking it up and sitting down on the edge of the bed. It's fat, stuffed with receipts and business cards that are clipped inside the cover and on various pages. "This is going to be my Bible."

Saying that out loud feels strange—especially since I spent so much time in prison reading the real Bible—but if I'm going to take over Eve's life without anyone figuring out what's going on, I need to brush up on who I am supposed to be.

I'm no longer Millie, the woman accused of murder.

I'm Eve. Grieving widow. Rich as can be.

Flipping the planner to tomorrow's date, I run my finger down the page.

"Looks like I have a full schedule." I chuckle when I see what I have coming up. "Not only do I have that nail appointment in the morning with Mya, but then I go to Pilates after a short break. Lunch at noon... but it doesn't say who I'm meeting."

I tap my finger against my chin, thinking hard. I expect that whoever I'm supposed to meet at Blue Sky will approach me when they see me arrive. I don't like that Eve didn't write down exactly whom I'm supposed to meet there, but it's not like I can go ask her.

The thought makes me laugh harder.

After putting the planner on the bed, I wander downstairs to get Eve's phone. That's what I'm going to use for an alarm, to make sure I don't oversleep and miss my appointment with Mya. I can only imagine how she'd react if I didn't show up.

Eve's cell phone is in her purse that she dropped by the front door when she came in. I pull the phone out, ignoring the lipsticks and wadded-up bills in the bottom of the bag.

With a quick tap on the screen, I turn it on, but my stomach sinks when I realize it's locked.

"What would you have as your passcode, sister?"

I walk into the kitchen with the phone and sit down at the counter, resting my elbows on the cool quartz countertop. "Our birthday, maybe?"

No, not that. I type it in anyway, not surprised when the phone remains locked. She's not that sentimental.

I look around the kitchen. Eve and Joe never had kids, so I can't try one of their kids' birthdays. On a whim, I type in Joe's birthday, but the phone remains locked.

"I know what it is," I whisper, then quickly type in the day of Joe's murder before I convince myself that I've lost my mind.

It works. The phone screen blanks out for a moment, and the next thing I know, I'm staring at her screen full of apps and icons. There are two missed calls, but I ignore those and click on her messages to see who's been texting her.

As confident as I am in taking over her life, the last thing I want to do is make a phone call as Eve right now. I need to make sure I have my head on straight and that I'm prepared for it.

"You were sick in the head, Eve, you know that?" I still can't believe she used the day and month she murdered Joe as her PIN. "Okay, what messages do you have?"

There's one from Mya making sure we're on for tomorrow morning. I type out a quick response to let her know I wouldn't miss it for the world.

Her response is immediate.

I hope Millie isn't going to be an issue. What are you going to do about her?

I can't believe her reply. "Are you serious right now?"
I close my eyes and take a deep breath, then fire off my response.

She's the worst, but she left town. I told her she wasn't welcome here.

Is Mya going to believe me?
There's a cold chill that has settled on my arms. I give a little shiver, trying to warm up, as I wait for a response. Maybe she just won't respond. Maybe what I said will be more than enough to get it through her head that I got rid of... well, me.
Her response takes a moment to come in.

Good. She seemed like a bitch.

"Wow." I breathe the word, a little surprised that Mya would say that about me when she doesn't even know me.
Whatever.

She's gone now

I respond, then close the texting app, hoping that will put an end to our conversation.
It does.
Now that Mya is out of the way until tomorrow, I tap on Eve's camera roll, interested to see if it will give me clues into my sister's life. Most of the pictures are selfies, which makes me roll my eyes, but as I scroll through them, I see pictures

she took of meals, of her with groups of friends, and of her lattes at the coffee shop.

"Okay, you're telling me my sister is basic," I mutter, flipping through the pictures.

There's nothing on here that clues me in as to who she is, and I'm getting bored looking through them. I'm about to tap away from the photos when I see a picture that doesn't make sense.

This makes me sit up straighter on the stool. I was slouching before, but I roll my shoulders back and shift a bit, still staring at the phone.

"What in the world are you?"

Using two fingers, I enlarge the image, tilting the phone a little bit to try to get a better angle on the picture. It doesn't matter how I turn the phone, nothing that I'm seeing right now makes any sense.

I've never seen this combination lock before, but it's right there on screen, zoomed out far enough that I can tell what it's attached to. A safe. I see fabric hanging loosely beside it, like someone pulled it back to see the safe better.

"Where in the world is this?" I get up, still holding the phone out in front of me, and walk through the house, going room by room as I look for the safe.

It's not downstairs.

My breath catches in my throat as I hurry up to the second floor. At the top of the stairs I pause, then walk into the room to the left, directly into Eve's bedroom.

Looking up from the screen, I see the huge tapestry Eve has hanging on the wall. It's totally out of place here, looking like it belongs in a castle not her house in Tennessee, but it's obvious in the photo that the safe is behind this particular tapestry.

I see from the photo that she pulled the tapestry back, as

if to show someone exactly where the safe is. I can't imagine why she would want to send that shot to someone.

Maybe she wasn't showing someone where it's located. Maybe she wanted proof that it's there.

I slip off the bed and walk across the room, the phone still in my hand and out in front of me. At the tapestry I pause, then reach out and grab the edge of it, fingering it before I pull it back from the wall.

It's heavy and thick and probably cost a small fortune. If the photo on the phone is real, then there will be a safe back here. It's probably just to keep her jewelry and some cash, but what if there's something more?

I finally get the tapestry pulled back far enough and gasp at the size of the safe. It's more than big enough for jewelry and cash, it's big enough for me to walk right in once I get the door open.

"Let's see how dumb you were." I slip the phone into my pocket and spin the dial on the lock. "Did you use Joe's death date for this code as well?"

I turn the dial, holding my breath, fully expecting to hear the click of the lock telling me that I cracked the code and that I'm in. I want to know what my sister has tucked away in her safe, and I feel an incredible need to get my hands on it right now.

But the date of his death doesn't work.

Stepping back, I let the tapestry fall back into place.

And that's when the doorbell rings.

15

MILLIE

WEDNESDAY

I almost don't answer the door, but I have to know who would show up to Eve's house without any warning. It's getting late, past the time when you would call on someone without calling first, and although part of me hopes it's Mya coming by to check on me, I have a nagging feeling that it's someone else.

Stopping in front of the door, I smooth down the front of my pajamas—like that's going to hide the fact that I'm in my pjs—and unlock the door. I step to the side as I swing it open. At the last minute, I remember how Eve leaned against the frame when I came to the house, so I do the same, adopting a scowl that matches the one she wore that day.

The man standing on the front porch eyeballs me, then brushes past me to enter the house.

I close the door and turn, to watch him cross the foyer to the stairs, and head up them.

"Excuse me," I say, shutting the front door and throwing the locks on it. "Can I help you?"

He turns to face me slowly, giving me ample time to look at him. The suit he's wearing looks tailor made. He has a strong jaw that's currently rigid. He stares at me as if he can't believe I would call out to him like this. I notice he's wearing black gloves and has a wrapped package in his right hand.

I look at it for a moment but can't make out what it is, and when he notices me staring, he tucks it under his arm.

"What did you say?"

The way his voice wraps around me like a wet blanket makes me shiver, but I shake off any insecurities and square off against him.

I survived prison. I can handle whoever this guy is.

"I asked if I could help you."

A moment later he's down the stairs, standing right in front of me, his eyes locked on mine.

He's tall, towering over me, with broad shoulders and a wide neck. For a man of his size, he moves a lot faster than I would have thought possible.

"You didn't pick up the phone, Eve. If you had, you would know I needed to drop something off upstairs."

I blink at him, needing to step back from him, but also well aware that the locked front door is right behind me, and there isn't anywhere for me to run.

"It's just like every other time, so there's no need to get high and mighty now. I'm going to drop it off. You'll babysit it for me, and when I'm ready for it, I'll come back and pick it up. Come on, you did such a good job yesterday with Rusty. Why do you have to ruin things now?" He grins, and the smell of his rancid breath washes over me, making my stomach churn.

Nervously, I pop the knuckles on one hand. It's a terrible

habit and one my mom tried to rid me of, but I never could stop.

Who the hell is Rusty?

"How long until you need it back?"

"Does it matter?" There's a sharp edge to his voice.

"No. I wanted to make sure that I'll be around. I didn't want to miss you." How did Eve know this man? He stares at me. My heart hammers out a staccato beat so loud in my chest that I'm sure he can hear it in the silence.

"You'll make sure you're here," he tells me, leaning forward and breathing me in.

I want to shiver away from him, want to put space between us. My body screams for me to move and get some distance, but there isn't anywhere I can go.

"You'll be here, Eve, or you know what I'll do."

I have no idea what this man will do to me, but he seems more dangerous than anyone I was locked up with. I was convicted of murder and met many women who actually deserved that title. This man looks like he'd be willing to murder anyone who stood in his way.

"I understand. I'm sorry," I tell him, hoping that an apology will suffice.

For a moment, he continues to stare at me; then he gives me a sharp nod before hurrying back up the stairs.

As soon as he's out of sight, I exhale hard and sink back against the front door. My knees feel weak, and I could easily sink down to the floor, but I manage to keep upright. I have no idea how long he'll be or what he might do if he sees me sitting on the floor.

I listen to the sound of him walking around in my bedroom, and then he appears at the top of the stairs. He walks down them slowly, as if he were taking a stroll in the park. With every step he takes, he stares at me, his eyes locked on me.

I stare at him, too, but not for the same reason. I need to keep my eyes on him, to make sure he won't move quickly or do something that will put me in more danger than I'm already in.

"There," he says, stopping in front of me and gesturing for me to move out of the way.

I do, but my feet are heavy.

"I'll be back for that later. It was lovely doing business with you, Eve." He unlocks the door and lets himself out.

As soon as it shuts behind him, I throw all three locks on the door and sag against it, my mind going a million miles a minute. When I hear a car door slam, I rush to a window and pull back the curtain to watch the car back down the driveway before leaving.

Across the road, I see a light on in Mitch's living room. Someone walks in front of the window, and I drop the curtain.

Hopefully they weren't watching what was going on. Hopefully they don't know about my visitor. I have no idea what he wanted, who he was, or what he left upstairs, but I need to find out.

It feels like I can't control my legs as I walk to the stairs and force myself up them. Any adrenaline that coursed through my body when the doorbell rang is gone, and I feel exhausted. My feet carry me into the bedroom, where I yank back the tapestry.

The lock is set; the door is shut. But he was here. I heard his footsteps in this room. I know he was tucking something away.

The only problem is I don't know how to get into the safe.

16

MILLIE

THURSDAY

Gripping the bottle of wine Mya brought over last night so tight that it doesn't accidentally slip from my hand and shatter on the ground, I walk up to the nail salon. I pull open the door, bracing for the smells and sounds of public life that are about to wash over me.

Public places are still too loud for me, too smelly. I'm used to some loud noises, sure, but not ones like this, where women are all chattering over each other, where there's laughter and music filling the air. I'm used to yelling and arguing, people getting in fights, guards screaming at everyone to be quiet, not piped-in music, nail polish, and women all happily gossiping.

I didn't leave the loud sounds of prison behind only to be thrust back into it once I got out into the real world. I knew it would be different, knew it would be difficult for me to focus and think when it was so loud all around me, but I never expected it to be this bad. I thought I'd have time to be by myself, to simply exist in my own quiet world.

So far, that hasn't happened.

Really, I thought that when I became Eve, my world would be quiet again, but it's been anything but that. There's so much noise, so many people wanting to see me, so many times I've wanted to be alone, yet I can't.

This is one of them.

"Eve!"

Mya's voice lifts above the din, and I glance over to where she's sitting—in a huge pedicure chair, her feet immersed in bubbling water, two empty glasses in her hands. "What are you waiting for? Get over here."

There's an edge to her voice, and I shiver. Smiling, I raise my hand in greeting.

"You can do this," I tell myself. "You can do hard things. You can face whatever it is that's going to happen to you. Remember, you survived prison."

After kicking off my heels, I sit down on the chair next to Mya. She moves both glasses to one hand, and I pass her the bottle of wine while I put my feet in the water. It's hot and bright pink, and I can't help the sigh that leaves my lips at how good it feels.

"What were you saying to yourself?" Mya hands the bottle of wine to a woman standing next to her. The woman opens it and fills the two glasses Mya's holding. Mya hands one to me. "When you walked in. It looked like you were muttering to yourself, but we both know how much you hate it when people mutter."

"Oh, there was a song on the radio, and I was trying to remember how it ends," I lie, taking a small sip of the wine. "This is very good," I say, wanting to change the subject. "What is it?"

Mya laughs, but the sound is tight. "You're insane, Eve. It's the same kind I bought when we started to work together, remember? It's our celebration wine. We made our agreement over this wine. It's a reminder."

"A reminder?" I swallow hard, trying not to think about what agreement she might be talking about, but even though I wish I could leave this salon and never look back, I also know I can't right now.

Mya is Eve's best friend, right? If she's not, then why did Eve spend so much time with her? Why in the world would she agree to hang out with Mya if they weren't good friends?

Unless it has something to do with the agreement Mya mentioned. I'm racking my brain, trying to come up with anything that might be reasonable, any clue that would tell me what my sister agreed to do with Mya.

And I'm coming up short.

"The last thing I want is for you to change your mind about anything." Mya's watching me like she's fully expecting me to argue with her.

I swallow hard. "What makes you think I'd change my mind?"

This makes her pause, and I feel heat flush up my neck. It obviously wasn't the right thing to say, but the words are out now, and there's nothing I can do to take them back.

"I saw your sister, Eve. I saw how much she looked like you, how happy she was to meet me, and it was obvious she wanted to spend time with you."

I'm sweating now, and I barely notice when the woman working on my toes twists bits of paper between them. She taps me on my knee, holding out her hand for something.

Polish. She wants polish.

There are a few bottles on the table between Mya and me. I grab one without paying attention to the color and hand it over to the woman.

Mya's eyes snap to the bottle and then back up to my face, but she doesn't say anything.

Did I choose the wrong color? Would Eve have worn something different?

"Millie's a bitch," I say, echoing the word Mya used last night to describe me. "I can't help that she's out of prison and so pathetic, but I did tell her to move on. To go to hell." I take a sip of my wine, thrilled that I managed to pick up my glass without my hand shaking.

Mya's eyebrow shoots up. "You think she left town? Just like that?"

I shrug, doing my best to look like I don't give a shit about what my twin is doing. "I think that if she knows what's good for her, she'll go. She may be out of prison, but that doesn't mean everybody thinks she's innocent. Trust me, she'll leave town."

"She'd better." Mya stares at me a moment longer, then rolls her head, cracking her neck. "Eve, we want this to work out between us, right?"

I nod. The wine goes down smoothly. Too smoothly. I should probably pace myself, but now that the glass is in my hand, and I've been sipping, it's hard to stop.

"Good. You're not going to do something we'll regret, are you?"

I shake my head. At the same time, I can't help but wonder what in the world she's talking about. It's clear Mya and Eve had a very different relationship to the one I thought they did when I first met Mya.

I thought they were best friends, but that's not what's going on here.

Not at all.

Mya doesn't act like a best friend. She's watching me with a look that is cold, calculating. I have a strong feeling that she's used to getting what she wants, and I'd better be willing to play the game.

Only I don't know what game she and Eve were playing. That's the problem.

"You sure you're okay? Not getting cold feet? Gareth will want to know. We all have to be on the same page to make sure this works."

Make sure what works?

If Mya wasn't Eve's best friend, then who the hell was she to her?

I think about the many appointments the pair kept during the week, and I feel my stomach twist.

"I think Millie rattled me, but that doesn't mean I'm not on board," I say, deciding to put the blame in a place I'm sure Mya will understand. There's no way I can tell her about the man who came to the house, or the safe in the wall, or the fact that Eve is dead and in the ground. *Surely she doesn't know all of that, right?* "Coming face-to-face with her like that shook me up. I thought I'd never see her again."

"You did your best for that to happen," Mya agrees, grabbing the bottle of wine to refill her glass.

I stare at her, taking in what she just said. She said something about that last night too, so it's obvious she knows that Eve framed me. But how involved was Mya? Was she in on it, did she help, or did she just hear about it from Eve after Joe was dead and I was locked up in prison? Mya wasn't Eve's alibi during the trial, but that doesn't mean she didn't know the truth.

"I did," I say, choosing my words as carefully as possible. "And I'd do it again."

"Even now?" Mya asks, lowering her voice and staring at me. "Knowing what you know now?"

What do I know now?

I pause, unsure of what to do, but then I finally force

myself to nod. It feels like someone else is using my mouth when I answer, "Even now."

She sits back in her chair, obviously satisfied, and gives me a nod.

"Good. I'm glad to hear that, Eve. You know, for the longest time, Gareth was afraid you were going to try to screw us."

"Gareth?" His name is unfamiliar, and my tongue feels clumsy saying his name. My voice sounds strangled, and I'm sure Mya is going to pick up on the tension.

"Yes, Gareth. He said you weren't yourself last night when he saw you, Eve. I assured him I'd see you this morning and talk to you, make sure everything was okay, but he was pretty upset. You'd never know it, of course, just looking at him, but he kept saying that something was off, that you were different. After I left your house, I called him, told him you were home. I wanted to check on you after you ran into Millie, and I was glad I did. I think he wanted to do the same thing."

I don't say anything. So Gareth is the man who came by last night. What did he have with him that he put in the safe? It's been driving me insane trying to figure it out. There's no way to know for sure unless I crack the safe and get in there myself.

Mya continues, "I promised him you wouldn't. I promised him you'd keep your head on straight, and I'm glad to hear that you will." When she looks at me, any bit of kindness I thought I saw on her face earlier is gone. Her mouth is tight, her eyes dark. She glares at me and then glances around the salon, as if to make sure nobody is listening in. "He was very worried."

She eyeballs me again, and I stare at her, suddenly unable to move. I don't think I could respond to her right now if I tried. I want to tell her that she's insane, that Gareth has obviously been watching too many movies if he thinks something strange was going on, but whatever words I want to use to explain disappear as soon as I feel able to speak.

Mya watches me in the same way an adult might look at some poor animal in a zoo. "So tell me, Eve, and be honest. You know that the two of us are always honest with each other. We have to be if this is going to work. Are you feeling yourself?"

17

MILLIE

THURSDAY

When I stumble out of the nail salon, I stop on the sidewalk. My eyes sting from the sun, my heart beats hard in my chest, my stomach churns. I might throw up.

Mya already left, leaving me to foot the bill—I watched as she strolled out the front door of the salon, her toes and fingernails shiny with polish. Now, I take a deep breath, bending over and grabbing my thighs to try to keep from passing out.

"She doesn't know," I say to myself. "She can't know. It's impossible that she or Gareth realizes that I'm not Eve."

My voice is low enough so that anyone who walks by shouldn't be able to hear what I'm saying, but the fear of being overheard still prickles the back of my neck.

There's no way Mya would have left the salon if she knew, right? She seems like the kind of woman who is used to getting her way, and I can't see her tolerating my lies if she has even an inkling of doubt that I wasn't telling the truth.

A woman walking past slows and glances at me; her eyes flick up and down my body. Did she hear me muttering to myself? Was she able to make out what I said?

What if someone does hear me? How many people in this town are close to my sister?

How many people in this town know what she did?

The thought is sobering, and I stand up, wiping my hands on my pants. I'm careful not to smudge my nails, but I check them over anyway, making sure they're perfect before I walk to my car.

Eve's car.

I thought this would be easy. I thought slipping into her little life would more than make up for the hell she put me through, but I'm beginning to wonder if I made a mistake becoming her. Eve wasn't quiet. She didn't have a small, simple little life for me to slip into and take over.

She knew things, but what's worse is other people know things about her.

I get in the car.

"Okay," I say, clearing my throat. The car is silent, small. It feels safe, like my cell in prison did, like my own hiding place where nobody can get to me, where nobody can hurt me. I can sit in here by myself and take the time to think things through, so I can figure out what I'm going to do next.

"Okay. What else do I have to do today?"

I flip open the planner I had tucked in my purse, grab a pen from the cupholder and strike through *nails with Mya*. It feels good to do that, so I strike through the words again, scribbling out her name in full, scribbling out the reminder that I was out with her.

With that done, I look at the note that says I have Pilates in an hour. My clothes are in the back seat of the car, so I could change in case the nail appointment ran long, but I'm on time. I can head home and relax for a minute before I have to come back out. I want to hide in the house and pretend this morning didn't happen.

But it did.

The engine growls to life, and I eat up the distance to home, driving as quickly as I dare. Next to me my phone is silent, but I keep expecting a phone call.

Expecting Gareth.

He doesn't call, but that doesn't stop me from glancing nervously at my phone. It feels dangerous, as though it is something I need to worry about coming to life and attacking me.

But the second I walk in the house, I relax. When I'm here, I feel like I can handle things. When I'm in the house, I feel like I have control over what's going on in my life. I know I don't, not really, but it feels safer here than it does out in town.

I'm halfway upstairs on my way to change when my phone rings. It's not a saved number, but I recognize it from last night.

"Hello?" My voice shakes a little when I answer the phone, so I try again. "Hello. This is Eve."

"I know who you are."

The familiar voice washes over me. *Gareth.* I stop and lean against the wall, my heart pounding.

"I heard your nails look nice. Was it fun?"

Swallowing hard, I close my eyes for a moment; then I answer, "So much fun, thanks for asking."

"Good. I need you to do something for me."

"What?"

"It's in the safe. I thought I'd be able to stop by today and pick it up, but I'm... busy. I need you to get the item out and bring it to me. Come now."

Inside, I'm screaming. Fear rushes through me at the thought of opening the safe and seeing what's in there. I can't let this man know that I'm scared, though.

"I can do that." I sound braver, and I'm grateful I do. Still, I'm sweating, and my body is shaking. "Where do you want me to bring it?"

"Our meeting spot. By the river."

The river. I know where the river runs through town, of course I do. How many times did I go swimming in it when I was younger? I loved going down there to dip my toes in the water when it was hot and to walk when I was stressed out. Eve hated it down there, always complaining that it smelled and that the mosquitos were bad.

"Of course. I'm sorry, I didn't sleep very well last night." I continue my walk upstairs, my feet on autopilot, leading me into the bedroom. "Do you just need the thing from last night?"

"That's it."

Is that amusement I hear in his voice? It's hard for me to tell because I can't imagine the man from last night ever being amused. Then again, I don't know him. All I know is how cold he made the house feel when he was in it, and how scared I was when he was close to me.

He might be the type of man who is amused when other people are scared.

"And the combination?" I close my eyes as I ask the question, sure that this will be the thing that undoes me. There's no way Eve didn't know how to unlock the safe, no way she didn't know the combination to it.

He's going to know I'm not Eve. It was insane of me to think I could do this. Just this simple question is going to clue him in that I'm a liar, and he's going to... well, I don't know what. But I know it's not going to be good.

There's a slight pause. I feel my skin grow colder as a new

wave of fear breaks over me. This is my undoing. He's figured out that I don't know anything. He has to know I'm not Eve.

"Six, sixteen, twenty-four, eighty-eight, nine."

"Six, sixteen, twenty-four, eighty-eight, nine." I repeat the combination, shock and relief flooding through my body. "Okay. I can do that."

"I'd hope so. I've always thought you were smarter than you looked, Eve. Get the item. Meet me at our spot. Now. And don't think for one moment that this means you have free access to the safe whenever you want. Open it without permission and I'll know."

He hangs up, and I rush to the tapestry, yanking it to the side to reveal the dial. My fingers shake as I grab it and start spinning it.

"Six," I say, my heart slamming hard. "Sixteen, twenty-four, eight-eight." One more number and I'll be in. "Nine."

I pause when I hear the click of the safe, then slowly turn the five-spoke handle to the right. The tumblers inside the safe shift and move, and the handle clicks into place.

Even though I don't want to open the safe and see what's in there, I know I don't have a choice. Putting my weight into it, I yank hard on the door. It moves slowly, feeling much heavier than I thought it would be, but it finally swings open.

If I didn't know the safe was here from Eve's photo, there's no way that I'd have found it.

It's completely hidden by the tapestry, and even when I close my eyes and try to concentrate, I can't picture exactly where I am in the house. How they managed to build such a large safe into the house without making it obvious from the first floor is beyond me.

I walk in, my heart thudding. It's not big enough in here for more than one person, but that's partly because of the shelves on both sides of the room. They have large boxes on them, each one heavy enough to bend the shelves a little in the middle. I reach out, trailing my fingers against their exteriors, fighting back the curiosity I have about opening them.

What in the world could Eve have locked in this safe?

No, not Eve. Gareth made it clear that I wasn't to be in the safe by myself, so it's obvious Eve didn't have access to it. If my sister was in charge of what was in the safe and what wasn't, then Gareth would have been shocked to hear that I don't know the combination to the lock.

My gaze drops to the floor and the package Gareth carried into the house last night.

Even without picking it up, I know what it is.

18

MILLIE

THURSDAY

Nobody's looking at me, but I can't help feeling like everyone is staring.

Joggers run by in bright T-shirts, headphones stuck in their ears, glazed expressions on their faces as they concentrate. Small kids run in circles around tired parents. I pass by a teenage couple in the midst of a breakup. Pathetic.

I barely give any of them attention as I walk past. My jacket pocket feels heavy, but nobody pays me any mind as I walk past them. Even though I know I haven't lost it, I keep dipping my hand into my pocket to make sure it's still there.

It is. I can't feel the metal through the cloth that's wrapped too thick around it, but I imagine I can. I jerk my hand back out of my pocket when an elderly couple walking with canes pass me.

Aware that I'm going to be late to my meeting with Gareth if I don't pick up the pace, I walk faster, constantly scanning for any sign of him or Mya. I doubt he'll be up here waiting for me if he said to meet him by the river, but part of me is convinced he'll be watching to make sure I don't mess up.

"Why would he worry about that?" I mutter. "He thinks you're Eve. Remember that. He doesn't know you're Millie, doesn't know you haven't a damn clue about what's going on."

Slowing, I turn off the main path through the park and cut through some trees that I know leads down to an opening by the river. This is where I used to come when I was in high school. The trees and brush have grown up since then, partially obscuring some of the path, but I pick my way through it quickly, grateful that the growth will likely deter other people from coming down here.

As soon as I walk into the clearing, I see Gareth, and I freeze. He looks bigger in the open than he was standing in the house, as if his body has expanded to fit the space around him. His back is to me, and his suit coat is pulled tight across his broad shoulders. I stare at him for a moment, thinking about what to do.

Finally, I clear my throat.

"Gareth?" My voice sounds thin in the open air, and I wince.

He turns to face me. I notice the slow smile spreading across his face. Unlike me, he comes across completely at ease. He's used to having little meetings in the woods.

"Oh, Eve, I was beginning to wonder if you were going to show."

I glance at Eve's watch. *My watch.* Eve must have known exactly what time to meet him. "I wanted to make sure nobody followed me down here." That seems like the right thing to say when you're toting a gun through the park, right?

He ignores what I said and walks over to me, closing the gap between us faster than I'm comfortable with. His quick moves make me want to step back from him, but I am frozen in place. The little voice that helped keep me alive in prison is screaming at me, wondering what in the world I'm doing with this guy.

This isn't smart. This is how people get murdered. I don't know anything about this guy, or what he and Eve did together, but I do know that I'm in it now, and I'm not sure how to get out.

"You know what a change of heart would mean for you, Eve. We have an agreement." Even though he hasn't threatened me outright, my stomach clenches.

"I know that," I say, pulling the gun from my pocket and offering it to him. "I was being extra careful today, that's all."

He takes the gun from me and shoves it into his jacket pocket without even looking at it. His eyes are still locked on my face, as if he is able to read my mind. "Mya is worried about you, Eve. Are you thinking about doing something stupid?"

Like killing my twin and burying her in the backyard?

I shake my head.

"You feel like yourself?" He's too close to me. I don't like people being so close that I could reach out and touch them. It's been a long time since I had my own personal space, and I have to fight to keep from taking a step back from him.

"I'm fine." My voice sounds thin again.

"Hmm. I hope so. I need you to make a drop for me this weekend." His voice rumbles through me, deep and gravelly, making the hair on my arms stand up straight. He pauses, stares at me, then continues, "Mya will be there to help you this time."

"Mya will?" I wonder if that's normal. I wonder if she used to go with Eve on drops, or if he's doing this as punishment because he doesn't like the way I've been acting. Unfortunately, there's no way for me to ask him without coming across as suspicious.

"Be ready, Eve. It's a doozy. She'll drop by around lunchtime on Saturday, so make sure you're ready to go." When he nods at me, I feel dismissed. When I take a shaky step backward from him, he stops me with a hand on my arm. "I'll be by yours tomorrow, and I'll need your help carrying some things into the safe. Make sure you're home."

I have to fight to dislodge my tongue from the roof of my mouth. It's stuck there, thick and dry, and I finally unseal it. "I will."

"Good."

He walks away from me, up the same path I came down to meet him. Halfway up, he starts to whistle, the sound thin and sharp.

I sink down to my knees and plant my hands on the ground. What the hell did I agree to? My head pounds, and my heart skips beats. Taking a slow breath in through my nose, I exhale hard through my mouth in an effort to clear my head. If I'm not careful, I'm going to pass out. Gareth's visit has left me feeling like I'm made of air, like my body isn't mine any longer.

"Okay, Millie, you've got this," I whisper to myself, standing back up. When I waver on my feet, I reach out for a tree to lean against. The bark bites into my skin, and I exhale hard again.

I'm alone in the woods. Gareth is the only person who knows I'm down here, and he's gone, but I still feel like someone might be watching me. My skin crawls with the thought, and I suddenly want nothing more than to be at home, with the door locked, buried under the covers on my bed.

I stumble up the path, forcing myself to take steps, even though my body is screaming at me to sit down and rest. I can't sit down. I have to keep going, have to get out of here. I don't think Gareth will come back to see me again, but what if he does?

What if he suddenly decides he's not finished with me, and he needs me to do something else? What if he wants me to use the gun I brought him? The thought is terrifying enough that I hurry up the shady path. When I step out into the sun, I gasp for air.

This part of the park feels so different than where I just met with Gareth. Some kids are playing in the grassy area in front of me, while others are being pushed on swings by their parents and some offered snacks. When a teenager flies by on his skateboard, I step back to get out of the way.

Being in the sun instead of the dark makes it feel like nothing bad just happened. I could easily pretend that I didn't have that meeting with Gareth, that I didn't show up to the park with a gun in my pocket.

Taking a deep breath, I start walking back to my car. My movements feel jerky and irregular, and I have to concentrate to move my arms and legs.

It feels like I'm being watched, but nobody is looking at me. I glance around, searching for that someone who might be paying more attention to me, but I don't see anyone. Everyone in the park is more interested in what they're doing.

Everyone except for one man.

I see the police cruiser before I see the officer walking across the park toward me. My stomach flips, and I feel nauseous. His sunglasses make it impossible for me to see his eyes, but I don't need to see them to know they're trained on me.

19

MILLIE

THURSDAY

"Eve!"

I hear my sister's name, know that it came from the police officer walking in my direction, yet I don't stop. In the back of my brain, there's a voice screaming at me to stop and talk to him before he gets upset, but I can't seem to stop. My legs are on autopilot, and I continue to put one foot in front of the other on my way to the park.

"Eve, stop!"

How long can I push this? I need to acknowledge him. My years of listening to wardens, doing exactly what they told me, making sure they were happy so they wouldn't punish me, finally kicks in. I stop, swallow hard, then turn to see the officer.

The closer he gets, the younger I think he is. There's a smile on his face, but I can't tell if it reaches his eyes, thanks to his sunglasses. Is he smiling because he's happy to see me or because he's happy that he's the one who found me? Does he know that I had a gun in my pocket just a short while ago?

"I thought you didn't hear me," he says, sweeping his glasses up and perching them on his head.

His smile definitely reaches his eyes.

The officer grabs my hand and squeezes it, and I'm struck by my first thought that he's cute.

Swallowing hard, I force a smile.

"I was in my own world, I guess." My eyes flick down to his badge. *Johnson.* Even while I smile, I'm thinking hard, trying to remember if I ever heard that name back when I went through my trial and was then put in prison. I'm not sure that I remember it.

He must be new. He must be a rookie who's chomping at the bit to find someone breaking the law in the park.

But then how did he know my name?

"You were like that a little bit last night, too, before you scooted out of our date early. Is everything okay?" Reaching out, he pushes some hair back from my face and tucks it behind my ear.

I freeze when his fingers linger on my cheek before he drops his hand. His eyes are locked on mine. He's waiting for me to speak, obviously interested in how I'm going to respond.

"Oh, things are fine," I tell him, putting two and two together.

I still don't know who this guy is, but Eve was with him last night. That must be where she goes on Wednesdays. There wasn't anything about it in her planner, but Mya made it clear Eve wasn't available Wednesday evenings.

It makes sense though when I think about it. Of course Eve wouldn't want Mya or Gareth to know what she was up to every Wednesday, especially if she was with a cop.

Shaking my head, I grin at him. "I don't know what's going on, maybe the weather?"

"You do tend to get pressure headaches." There's that smile again, completely disarming. "I was surprised to see you out here, knowing how you prefer to spend your time inside when the weather changes so rapidly." His gaze drops to my legs. "You have dirt on your jeans. Did you fall?"

I'm learning so much about Eve by talking to this guy, but I still have no idea who he is. He obviously knows more about her than I do, so I must pay attention to whatever he's saying, but I'm still confused.

"No, I'm fine," I say, doing my best to quickly collect my thoughts. "It was so nice and sunny out today I wanted to come out and walk around." I shrug, trying to look casual. "I simply couldn't bear being inside when the day was so inviting."

"Who are you, and what have you done with Eve?" he asks, laughing. "I definitely remember offering to take you to the beach for our anniversary next month and you telling me that you didn't want to spend time in the sun unless you had to."

We have an anniversary?

"I don't know," I say, forcing a laugh. "Something about it hit me right this morning, and I realized I wanted to be outside. I'm sure it will pass, don't worry." I lightly touch his arm. We're obviously in a relationship, and that's what people do, right?

Yes. It is the right thing. The officer smiles at me and puts his hand over mine before linking our fingers together and giving mine a little squeeze. There's a sweet smile on his face, and I can't help but wonder how someone like him got tangled up with Eve.

There's no way she'd ever go for a nice guy like this. She's too cunning, too cruel, yet she was obviously dating this man.

I grin at him, then pull my hand away. Before things get too chummy, I need to figure out what I'm going to do about Mya and Gareth.

"I'll let you get back to work," I tell him, smiling to soften the blow of letting go of his hand. "I know you have a busy day solving crimes, so don't let me stop you."

He rolls his eyes, but it's good-natured. "You know how it is. Alex this, Alex that. Arrest this person, Alex. Make sure you check out the park. That's actually why I'm here."

A chill runs up my spine. "Why are you here, Alex?" I try his name out, and I'm pleased when he smiles at me. "I'm out for a walk, but you don't normally get to take a break in the middle of your shift, do you?"

"No, but there was a report of a strange guy here, so I said I'd come and check it out." Turning away from me, he glances around behind him before facing me again. "Did you see anyone who might prompt a stay-at-home mom to call us in a tizzy?"

Gareth.

I shake my head. "Nope. Like I said, in my own world." I tap the side of my head to get the point across and pretend to look around us with concern. We're not going to see Gareth—of that much I'm sure. He's long gone, crawled back under whatever rock he lives beneath.

And thank goodness. It hits me that he might catch me talking to a cop. That thought forces me to take another step back from Alex.

That's why Eve doesn't have any messages from this guy in her phone. That's why he doesn't even *exist* in her phone. The last thing she probably ever wanted was for Gareth or Mya to see him pop up as a contact.

"Well, I'm going to walk around and look for him. You be safe." He leans in quickly—much faster than I do—to kiss me before I can pull back. His lips are soft and warm when they brush against mine, and then it's over.

"I shouldn't do that when I'm in uniform," he tells me, winking, "but I couldn't resist. Talk to you later, Eve."

"Bye, Alex." His name feels strange on my tongue. I watch him walk away for a minute before I shake my head to clear it and turn back to my car.

It makes absolutely no sense that my sister would want to date someone like him. He's way too nice for one thing, and he's a cop for another. She probably had to creep around, doing everything she could to keep her relationship a secret from Gareth and Mya.

It sounds exhausting.

"I can't do that," I say to myself as I get in the car and crank it. The engine turns over. I angle the vents so the air conditioning blows right in my face. "No way can I keep dating that guy."

He's cute, but that doesn't matter right now. Things are too confusing with Gareth and Mya and all the things they want me to do for them. I'd rather have those two out of my life first, but there's no way I'm going to get rid of them easily.

"I don't know what I'm going to do about him," I say, pulling out of the parking lot.

Alex is standing by his police car when I drive by, and he waves at me. I lift my hand in return, a fake smile on my face.

"He seems nice, but I might have to break up with him."

Sounds easy. Break up with the cute cop my sister was dating and somehow manage to keep Gareth and Mya at bay. I don't know how that will work, but I also can't imagine continuing to date him and keeping them from finding out the truth. My other option is to turn them over to Alex, but I can't see how that's possible.

Not when there's a giant safe full of drugs and guns in my

bedroom. Not when I'm pretty sure I saw a box of jewelry tucked in the back. It has to be stolen, right? Alex may love Eve, or think he does, but I have a pretty good feeling he'd turn me in in a heartbeat if he knew what was in my bedroom.

No, I have to get rid of Alex, have to push him away. I don't want him getting hurt, but at the same time, there's no way I'll go back to prison. I'll do anything to keep that from happening.

Anything.

20

MYA

SATURDAY

I arrive at Eve's house well before lunch, and I ring the doorbell three times, then bang on the door before stepping back and waiting.

I could let myself in. I finger the key I have to Eve's house in my pocket. Gareth and I both have a copy, but we try not to use them. Eve knows that she needs to be available to us whenever we need her.

When she doesn't answer, I ring the bell one more time, wanting to get my point across.

The last thing I want is to give her a chance to pretend she didn't hear me. She has to hear me no matter where she is in that ridiculously big house of hers. I keep telling Gareth that I want something bigger than this one day. He tells me not to be naive, that big houses attract attention, and the reason we've been able to operate without getting caught for so long is because we fly under the radar.

Screw flying under the radar. I want a walk-in closet like Eve has.

Raising my fist, I prepare to knock again. Then the door swings open, and Eve glances through the crack; her eyes widen.

"Mya, it's you," she says, opening the door the rest of the way.

"Who the hell else were you expecting, Santa Claus?" Planting one hand on the door, I push it open, shoving her out of the way in the process. When I walk into her foyer, I take a deep breath. Her house always smells good, as if she has candles burning all the time. But I can't put my finger on what the scent is.

It isn't until she locks the door and steps in front of me that I get a good look at her. She's wearing jeans, a black T-shirt that fits her like it was made for her, and a pair of sneakers. She's put together, as always, and it hits me again how much I dislike this woman. It hasn't been easy spending so much time with her, not when I hate her.

Someone had to do it. Someone had to make her think they were on her side before turning her world upside down. Someone had to show her what would happen to her if she didn't cooperate.

The pedis, the wine, the laughter out in public... they're not because I like spending time with Eve. Someone needs to keep her on a short leash. Gareth was worried at first that she would try to go to the cops to get out of our arrangement, but she hasn't ever tried. She's afraid, and for good reason.

We told Eve exactly what we do to people who turn on us.

"What are we doing today?" She rubs her hands together and then drops her arms by her sides in an attempt to look nonchalant.

"We have some items to drop off," I tell her. "Gareth is

taking care of other business right now, so you and I have some things to do. Come on, we need to get into the safe."

Eve normally follows me up the stairs, but this time she leads the way, hurrying up them.

I take my time, watching her as I go. Gareth mentioned that she seemed a little off at the park, that he couldn't quite put his finger on what it was. I sense it too. But I don't know what it is.

She was equally off when we had our pedicure on Thursday, but she explained that it was due to her sister getting out of prison. I believed her, but I'm still going to keep an eye on her.

I still need to make sure she isn't going to do something rash.

In the bedroom, Eve walks over to the huge wall tapestry and pulls it out of the way, giving me plenty of room to open the safe. I take my time, watching her expression closely as I turn the dial and enter the combination. She's watching my moves but with a blank expression, like she's seen this done a thousand times, not like she's actually interested.

Gareth mentioned that he gave her the combination to the safe the other day. I was pissed. Why the hell did he do that when the arrangement of me and him having the combination has worked fine up until now? I don't know, but you don't argue with Gareth.

Not if you want to keep living, anyway.

"You feeling okay?" I ask Eve when I pull the safe door open and gesture for Eve to drop the tapestry and walk inside.

She does, nodding as she passes me.

"Yeah, I'm a little tired, I think. I don't know what it is, but I can't seem to shake it." As an afterthought, she adds, "Maybe it's the change in the weather."

"Maybe."

She stands to one side in the safe while I grab two backpacks from hooks on the wall and begin filling one. We don't need a lot of things today, just some of the money and drugs. I load the money in one backpack and the drugs in another. Eve always carries the drugs when we do drops like this. It's best this way, and the only good way to make sure she doesn't cross us.

She takes the backpack from me and slips it on her back. "Anything else?"

"No." We leave the safe, and I lock it before she lets the tapestry fall back in place.

I face her. "You don't seem like yourself, Eve. I hope you're not having any doubts. No regrets. We hope you're not thinking about refusing to work with us any longer, because you know what would happen if you did that."

She swallows hard and doesn't say anything.

"You do know, don't you, Eve? Do I need to remind you?"

"I know," she says, her voice timid.

"You know that we'll turn you in for having Joe killed," I say, wanting to drive the point home. "All of this, your house, your money—it will be gone. Millie's out of jail, and who do you think they're going to come looking at next?"

Her head snaps up. "My alibi is airtight," she argues. "That's not an issue. There's no way anyone would ever be able to convict me."

"Maybe, maybe not." I shrug, because I don't care what happens to her. "But I have a very good feeling that you wouldn't like being in jail while they figure that out, am I right? I can't imagine that would be fun for anyone. Should we call Millie and ask her what she thinks?"

Eve stares at me, anger burning in her eyes. "Millie is gone. I told her to get out of town, and she did."

"Just like that?" I snap my fingers.

"Just like that." Eve doesn't blink. "She's gone, so whatever concerns you still have about her or about me are unfounded. I've got this, just like I've always had it when you needed me."

It's the same thing she said to me Wednesday. I wasn't inclined to believe her then, but I looked for Millie and couldn't find her around town.

Maybe Eve is telling the truth. She'd better be.

"That's rich for you to think that we really need you, Eve. You think that we couldn't replace you?" She doesn't respond, so I start walking toward the stairs. "Believe me, you're useful, but that doesn't mean we couldn't find someone else to be just as useful, got it?"

"I got it."

We walk down the stairs and return to the front door. I lead the way outside and wait while she locks the door. She does, twice, and puts the key in her pocket.

"You didn't lock the top lock," I point out, watching her expression.

She lifts her chin and stares at me, like she's trying to prove how tough she is.

Then she blinks hard.

"I forgot." Eve turns back to the door and pulls the key from her pocket. The top lock slides into place quickly with a soft snick. She faces me again, shoving the key into her pocket once more. "There. I'm ready now."

"Go get in the car."

I point to my SUV and watch her as she hurries to do just that. She's not looking over her shoulder at me, but she has to know I'm watching her. She moves quickly, like she wants to please.

That's great. I love it when she gets her ass in gear, when she does what I tell her to do.

But there's just one problem.

In all the years I've been working with Eve, she's never once locked that top lock.

21

MILLIE

SATURDAY

I keep my face turned toward the window for as much of the drive as possible. Mya keeps glancing over at me—I see her head move out of the corner of my eye—but the last thing I want is to talk to her.

Fear eats at me when I think about starting a conversation with her. Gareth already picked up that something was different with me, and there's no way for me to know if I'm doing everything the same as Eve would. Pretending to be my sister is a lot harder than I thought it would be.

Spreading my hands out on my thighs, I look down at them. My nails are gorgeous, manicured, polished. They look like the nails of someone who has their life together, not someone like me, not someone who killed her sister.

This was supposed to be easy. The hard part was getting rid of Eve, and now I'm here, supposed to be enjoying her life of luxury.

Instead, I have a backpack full of drugs tucked between my feet while a stranger drives me to God knows where in a black SUV. Taking a deep breath, I risk a look at Mya.

Her jaw is set. Determined. She has one hand draped casually over the steering wheel. The other is tapping out the rhythm to a song on her leg only she can hear. The first time I saw her, I thought she looked so friendly, that she was someone I definitely wanted in my life. Now, of course, I know better. I see the lines around her eyes, the tight way she holds her mouth, even when I get the feeling she's meant to be relaxed.

When she realizes that I'm looking at her, she fixes her gaze on me, one eyebrow perfectly arched. "What?"

"Nothing. I didn't know how much longer we're going to be in the car. Are we just dropping this stuff off?" That seems like a fair question. I'm trying to frame everything I ask as how Eve would. If I think she would ask the question, then I ask it. If I don't think she would, then I won't allow those words to leave my lips.

It's the best strategy I have right now. I'm not sure how in the world I'm going to keep Mya and Gareth from figuring out that I'm not my sister. They're obviously a little suspicious already, and that worries me. If I can learn quickly, though, if I can take whatever steps are necessary to play this role without them finding out the truth, then I think I'm going to be okay.

Never mind the fact that I don't know my sister nearly as well as I thought I did. I never would have imagined that she'd be involved in something like this.

Whatever this is.

And never mind that I keep making mistakes and making Mya and Gareth more and more suspicious about what's going on with me.

I either have to be careful about asking questions in my

attempts to get more information about Eve and her relationship with these pair or keep my mouth shut. Knowing Eve... well, she wouldn't have done the latter. She would have talked, would have questioned, would have wanted to know what was going on.

Right?

"We're almost there." Mya smiles at me, showing more teeth than is natural, then looks back at the road. "What's with your endless supply of questions today, Eve? You don't seem like yourself."

Okay, I was wrong.

I can be quiet. I'll shut my mouth from now on and only speak when Mya speaks to me. That's probably the best option I have right now anyway, the only way that I can stop putting my foot in my mouth.

I'm freezing, even though the sun is shining through the window and warming my arm. It's not because of a chill in the air that makes me cold. I can't shake the feeling that I'm going to slip up, and Mya and Gareth will realize I'm not Eve.

Will they kill me then? Would they give me time to explain? I have no idea, but I don't want to find out.

It's only when we pull off the main road and onto a dirt side road that I look ahead to see what's going on. Mya drives more slowly now, carefully navigating the ruts in the road. We bounce around in the car when she hits one.

"Okay," she says, parking between two large trees. "Here we are. Bring the backpack, Eve, and don't talk. Nobody likes it when people talk too much at these things." She eyeballs me, and I nod, unsure of what else I should do.

What a joke. If there were anything else I could do right now, I'd do it, but I'm caught. Mya knows it. I know it. I don't want to get out of the car with her, but it's not like I have a choice. Whatever life Eve was living before is mine now, and I have to figure out how to play along until I can come up with a plan to get rid of Gareth and Mya.

I step out of the car. My backpack is heavy, and I adjust it.

Mya joins me, her own pack tight on her back. She tips her chin at the woods ahead. "It's a short hike, and I know that's not your thing, so I'm glad you left the stilettos at home." Without waiting for a response, she leads the way.

I follow, unable to do anything else. There's a voice in my head screaming at me that I'm going to die here, but I try to push it down and make it shut up. She won't kill me, right? She wouldn't make me come all this way to drop off these drugs and then kill me.

Right?

My mouth feels dry. I swallow hard as I follow her along the path through the woods. It would be the ideal afternoon for a walk if I weren't so afraid of what awaits the two of us. My foot catches on a root, and I stumble. Mya glances over her shoulder at me, and I think she's going to tell me to catch up. But she doesn't seem to notice or care that I'm having a little trouble.

The woods thin out, and I'm surprised to see a small cabin in the middle of a clearing. It's not a shanty exactly, although it definitely doesn't look like the type of place I would want to visit when on vacation. There are two men standing in front of it. They stop talking to each other and look at us when Mya and I walk up.

"You made it." One of the men glances at Mya, then flicks his gaze to me. "I wasn't sure you were going to be on time."

"You're the one who chose the meeting spot in the middle of nowhere." Mya slips her backpack from her shoulders, and I follow suit, keeping hold of it in one hand while the two of them talk. "This is Eve. You'll be dealing with her a lot going forward. I have other things to do."

The man grunts. It sounds like a signal. The other man

disappears into the house, then returns with a small bag that he hands to Mya.

"Drugs and money," Mya says, gesturing for me to hand my backpack over.

I do, keeping my hand back so I don't accidentally touch the man. He grabs the bag from me and unzips it, then looks inside before zipping it back up and nodding.

"And for you." The man gives Mya a package. She doesn't open it, doesn't even pay attention to it as she tucks it under her arm. "We'll be in touch when we get this lot sold. Hopefully sooner rather than later."

"I'll have to see how quickly I can get my hands on more pills. It's not easy to get them without drawing suspicion." Mya sounds rueful, and I glance at her.

What in the world does she do? I want to ask her where she gets the drugs, but I'm not stupid enough to speak up. The best thing to do right now is stay as quiet as possible and hope I don't draw attention to myself.

"We'll be in touch," the man repeats. "Tell Gareth it's always a pleasure doing business with him." He looks at me again, his gaze skating over my body. I feel a flush start on my chest and work its way up to my cheeks, making them burn. "Can't wait to work with you, Eve."

I don't answer. I can't answer.

But then Mya turns to me, her eyes wide. She nods her head at me, as though it's my turn to speak.

"I'm looking forward to it," I lie.

I'm sure he sees through my lie, and when he smiles, the sight of his crooked teeth makes my stomach twist.

Before things can get more uncomfortable, Mya grabs my arm and turns me around to face the way out. She plants her hand in the middle of my back and pushes me down the trail back to the car.

When we reach the car, she turns to me. "You pick now to

stop talking? Jesus, Eve, were you trying to get us killed?" Her eyes are dark, and she stares at me, then slams her hand on the hood before she gets in the driver's seat.

I stand still for a moment before reaching for the handle. A thought washes over me as I watch her slip the key into the ignition. I wasn't trying to get us both killed, no.

In all of this, Eve was the only person who was supposed to get hurt.

Maybe I'm going to have to take care of Mya and Gareth in order to get what I really want.

I have to decide if I'm ready to do that.

I'm pretty sure I am.

22

MILLIE

SATURDAY

After the meeting in the woods with Mya and the strange men, I just want to go back to bed, but I force myself to shower and pull on some clean clothes. I want to enjoy my new life—Eve's life—even though I'm exhausted.

Going to bed and moping is not the best way to enjoy your life. While it sounds good, I grab the car keys instead, get in the car, buckle up, and start the engine.

I'm shell-shocked. I keep looking at my hands like I can't believe they're mine, like I can't believe what I've done with them. I never thought that this perfect life would spiral out of control the way it has.

This is surreal, and even though I want to curl up under a blanket and pretend like none of it is happening, I refuse to do that. I refuse to let Eve win.

Even though I have no idea what to do, and no idea

whom I can trust, I don't want to stay at home. It's not safe here, not with Mya and Gareth wanting access to the house and safe at all times.

I need to get out.

But I have no idea where to go. I don't want to go to the park and walk around, running the risk that I might run into Gareth or someone who saw me there with him on Thursday. My stomach turns when I think about the officer I met.

Alex.

He seemed like such a nice guy, definitely the kind of person I would go for. I don't know what in the world Eve was doing with him. He's not her type, not at all, or at least, he wasn't the type of guy she'd go for when we were younger. He seems kind, thoughtful—everything a man should be.

I glance over at my phone in the cup holder, thinking about how much I would love to call him and suggest we go out on a date. But I have no way to get in touch with him.

I'm certainly not going to call the police department and ask for him by name.

Even if I knew how to get in touch with Alex, it wouldn't be smart. I need to stay as far away from him as possible, no matter how much I think we would be a good match.

He can't know about Gareth and Mya, and of the three of them, I have a pretty good idea he'd be the one to tell that I'm not Eve.

"You're going to have to find your own fun," I tell myself, gritting my teeth and backing down the driveway. "When's the last time you went shopping, anyway? Doesn't matter, now's the first time that you actually have money to burn and a great body to dress."

With that thought in mind, I drive quickly across town, skipping the little department stores I would have frequented before, then pull up in front of a chic clothing store called Azalea Park. Before going to prison and becoming Eve, I never would have looked twice at this place. It's out of my budget.

Rather it was, but it isn't anymore.

A rich floral scent hits my nose when I open the door. My wide gaze travels over the racks of expensive clothes and the thin women who are dressed for a trip to the country club. I notice the employee's eyes darken when she sees me standing in the door.

"Eve, to what do we owe this pleasure?" she asks, crossing her arms and walking over to me.

I drop my gaze to her chest to look for a name tag, but there isn't one to be found.

"I thought I'd come see about updating my wardrobe," I say, putting a charming smile on my face.

The woman doesn't appear charmed. "Your money is always welcome here," she says, giving me the distinct impression that it's me who's not welcome, "but you will not have one of my staff help you pull clothes, not after you made Anna cry last time."

"About that," I say, wanting to smooth over whatever it was that my twin did. "I wanted to apologize. I don't even have to shop here if you'd rather I go, but I want to say that I'm sorry. There's no excuse for my behavior."

The surprised look on the woman's face is gone almost as quickly as it appears, but I saw it. I know it was there.

I thought I'd learn a lot about Eve by getting closer to Mya and Gareth and learning how the three of them interacted, but I think I'm seeing an entirely different side to her. She has this nice guy she's dating, but the women in this boutique obviously hate her.

"That's good of you, and I'll tell Anna, but that doesn't mean you're welcome here, Eve. We don't need you and certainly don't need your bitchy attitude."

The customers in the store are all focused on us. Nobody

moves. They're watching, listening, waiting to hear what's going to be said next. My face burns hot under the makeup I put on this morning, and all I want is to melt into the floor so I can pretend this public dressing-down isn't happening.

I nod. "I understand. And I'll be going, but please tell her how very sorry I am, okay?"

Most of the time, an apology will soften someone up, but the woman I'm talking to doesn't seem swayed by how terrible I feel. She gives me a quick nod, but there isn't any smile on her face. It's painfully obvious how ready she is to have me leave.

"I never thought I'd see the day when Eve Overstreet would come into this shop to apologize. We've been waiting a long time."

I swallow hard. "I know, and I'm not proud of the things I did in the past. I'm not proud of how I treated people, but I'm trying hard to turn over a new leaf and be the type of person I *can* be proud of. I hope each of you has a great day."

Without waiting for a response, I turn and leave the store, My heart is slamming in my chest. I feel the tears fall, but I don't reach up to wipe them away. Instead, I slip on a pair of oversized sunglasses I found in Eve's purse.

So my sister was cruel, and not only to me. But it sounds like she was trying something new out by dating Alex. I still can't picture my sister with him, can't imagine that she would be happy with someone as kind and calm as he seems to be. When we were younger, she was a force of nature, a hurricane tearing through the world, and she always hurt people who got swept up in her life.

I hated how she was from the time we were little, and it looks like some things never changed with age.

"Okay, no shopping, then," I say, pulling my keys from my purse and walking toward my car. Sure, I could try somewhere else, but the last thing I want is the same frosty reception at another store. No, even though all I wanted was to get out of the house and enjoy a little retail therapy, the best thing I can do now is go home.

I'm winding my way through the parking lot to my car when I see a flash of white fabric in front of me. A woman is loading her dry cleaning into the back seat of a very stylish SUV. She slams the door and looks around the parking lot.

It's so odd to see her in a place like this that I almost don't recognize her. Then I do.

Mya doesn't see me. She's too focused on getting in her car. I pause, then duck behind the car next to me. As my heart picks up the pace, I mentally run through my options, trying to decide what in the world I'm going to do.

I shouldn't follow her. That is most definitely the last thing I should do right now. What I should do is get in the car and go back to the house, lock the door, and pretend that none of this terrible day ever happened.

But I can't shake the feeling that I need to get to know her better. I need to learn what makes her tick, why she and Gareth are doing this, what they're hoping to accomplish. I have to figure out exactly what it is they want from me.

It has to be more than running little errands for them, right?

A part of me is convinced that if I follow her, I'll be able to figure out exactly how much she knows about me. That's why, even though the voice in the back of my head is screaming at me that I'm making a terrible decision, I get in my car and crank the engine, put on my seatbelt, and follow her out of the parking lot.

23

MYA

SATURDAY

I've got too much on my mind and not enough downtime to figure out what I'm going to do next. Stress eats at me as I pull out of the busy parking lot and gun it when I hit the main road. I hang a hard left at the green light right before it turns yellow.

The little voice in my head is screaming at me to slow down and be more careful, but I can't seem to do that. I want to drive fast; I want to speed through these curvy roads that wind their way around the mountains. I want to do whatever it takes to feel like I'm more in control of everything that's going on.

"Incoming call from Gareth," my car tells me. I answer it, barely glancing at the built-in screen on the dash. I know where every button in this car is, know exactly where I have to reach and what to press to get the car to respond to me.

"Mya, what are you doing?" His voice is warm and low, and it fills the car. I shiver into it, enjoying the way it wraps around me. Most people wouldn't understand why I feel the way I do about Gareth. He's dangerous, deadly.

But only for me, never against me. That's what makes this different than being with other men who want to be dangerous and scary. Sure, Gareth terrifies other people, but not me. He's never once been unkind to me. He's powerful, but uses that power to take care of me.

"Just picked up my dry cleaning," I tell him, glancing behind me in my rearview mirror when a small movement catches my eye. "You know how hard it is to keep white things clean."

He chuckles. "I'm going to be home late. I have to finish up this plan to get more suppliers under us. Will you be okay for dinner?"

"Of course I will." Before, it bothered me that he wasn't going to be home for the evening. I hated it that I wasn't going to get to see him before I went to bed, but now I know better than to get upset. Everything Gareth does is for me.

Including blackmailing Eve to make sure she helps out with our business.

"Good. How did it go with introducing Eve as the new contact today? Did they give you the package?"

The package.

I put it under the driver's seat and then forgot I even had it. My stomach sinks when I think about it there, exposed, ready for anyone to come along and see it.

"Things went fine," I tell him, adjusting my course away from my house toward Eve's. "She was fine. Chatty all of a sudden. I didn't like it."

I didn't like it doesn't come close to how much I hated Eve's inquisitiveness. It wasn't like her at all.

"Nervous?" I hear him swallow, and it's clear he's drinking a little whiskey while he works. Gareth isn't someone who drinks to excess, but he and I both know that sometimes a little alcohol makes putting plans together that much easier.

"Could be." I shrug even though there's no way he can see me. "I have no idea. I just didn't like it, and it may have weirded out the guys. Still, I think they'll be fine. They're professionals."

"How about this," he says, and I can already guess what he's going to ask me to do. "Why don't you go by Eve's house and see where she's at, mentally? It might be a good idea to remind her that we have all the power here and that we would be more than happy to leak some information about her killing Joe to the police."

I don't mention that Eve would be able to incriminate us if we did that. But Gareth is smart. He's already thought of that. He knows that we have to do whatever it takes to keep Eve under our thumb and willing to work for us, even if that means showing a few of the cards we hold.

"I'm actually one step ahead of you," I say, turning into Eve's neighborhood. Maybe that's the wrong word to use. There are only half a dozen houses here; the neighbors are spaced out from each other so everyone has privacy. Hers is tucked in the cul-de-sac, the closest neighbor is the one directly across from her house. As I drive closer, I scan the property for any signs of movement.

Nothing.

"Take care of it. Whatever her problem is, make sure she knows that we can be a bigger problem."

"I've got it. See you later."

Before he can tell me again to handle things with Eve, I press the red button in the middle of the screen to end the call. For a moment, I sit in the driveway with my car idling.

Then I kill the engine, grab the package from under the seat and get out, rushing up to the front door.

With the package tucked under my arm, I ring the door-bell and step back from the door. I expect Eve to open the door as soon as I ring the bell, but the door remains closed. Locked.

How many times have Gareth and I told her she's supposed to be here?

"What the hell?" I ring the bell again, then pull the spare key from my pocket. Eve's in there, she has to be. I can't imagine what else she'd be doing after this morning's meeting in the woods. She was stressed, that much was clear, but I don't think she's so desperate as to try to run.

When she doesn't answer the second bell, I let myself in, locking the door behind me before I hurry up the stairs to her bedroom. At the time when Gareth had this safe installed, I thought it was overkill, but it's filling up quickly. The tapestry rests heavy on my back as I open the door. I put the package inside and lock it back up.

Guns. Drugs. Money. Some jewelry. We deal in things that are difficult to get. Or illegal. That reminds me that I need to get more drugs, make sure we have enough on hand for when we need them.

I also need to find Eve. Gareth will be angry if I don't talk to her about her behavior this morning, and the last thing I want is for him to be upset with me. Pausing for a moment, I glance around her bedroom. It's always the same, always neat and picked up, but this time there's a pair of underwear tossed casually on the floor near the hamper, not in it.

I frown. Strange.

Eve is a bit of a clean freak, which is part of the reason why we like working with her so much. She's not the type of person to be messy and make a mistake. Still, she was rattled this morning, so the underwear on the floor probably has to do with nerves.

Shaking my head, I leave the room and walk back downstairs, making sure to swing through the kitchen and check everything is in place there. Last, I reach the front door.

My hand is on the lock, ready to unlock it, when the doorbell rings.

24

GARETH

SATURDAY

Mya opens the door, looking confused to see me standing on the front porch.

"What are you doing here?" Her tone isn't accusatory, mostly surprised. I kiss her before she moves out of the way to let me into the house. "I thought you had things to do. You didn't have to come. I told you I'd take care of it."

"Something's up. I don't like that she's making you nervous, and I think we need to talk to her." I look around the house, taking in the rich furnishings, the expensive art on the wall, the perfectly polished wide planks of wood that make up the stairs. "Do you think she loves it here?"

"Who?" Mya looks confused and glances around the house. I get the feeling she's trying to figure out what I'm going on about.

"Eve."

Now she crosses her arms and glares at me.

"I don't know what the hell you're going on about, Gareth, but it's time to spit it out. Yeah, I think she likes it here, probably a lot better than she'd like a jail cell, which is why she's so willing to work with us."

"Sure, but the woman you saw today, she's not Eve."

She stares at me like I've lost my mind, then finally barks out a laugh. "You're insane."

"It's not. It's her twin. Millie."

Again she laughs, but this time it's not as convincing as it was a moment ago. She keeps laughing until she sees my dead-serious expression; then she stops. "Wait a moment. You're serious. You think what... that Eve left town and let Millie take over for her? That's insane, that's what that is. Nuts."

I love it when Mya gets flustered. The two of us are a great pair, but she can't wrap her mind around things that have moved one step ahead of her. Or in this case, at least two.

"Eve's gone." I want to drive my point home to her. "This woman? She isn't Eve. She's Millie."

Mya stares at me, her eyes wide. "Seriously, Gareth, there's no way. That's... it's insane, that's what it is." She stares at me, and I watch as the realization slowly dawns on her. She sees it now, even though she didn't a moment ago. "I just thought Eve was a little off."

There are so many hints that are now leading me to believe we've been working with Millie all along, not Eve. It's the little things about her, stuff she did or said that are adding up against her.

The Wednesday night she was home, for one. She's never home on Wednesdays and made it clear when we first started working together that she couldn't be. For her to be home and then to act so strangely when Mya and I both went over there... something isn't right.

Her reaction wasn't right. Her mannerisms were off—how

she acted tough but didn't really seem tough. It wasn't the same woman I had just spoken to on the phone, I'm sure of it. She had no idea who I was when I went upstairs to the safe.

Sure, she let me go, but what choice did she have? It was obvious Millie was scared, and that's good.

She should be.

Mya's mentioned to me a few times that Eve has seemed off, but she doesn't want to see it. I can see the big picture. She can't. But I'll show her soon enough.

She inhales sharply, her eyes wide. "She locked all three of the locks that one time."

I nod, about to tell her everything, when the front door swings open. We left it unlocked, and the woman calling out sounds uncertain. "Hello?"

Millie obviously couldn't get her car into the garage with ours parked in the driveway. I grin at the thought of her being forced to come through the front door, knowing she's in trouble, but not knowing what's waiting for her.

"How about we get our answer now?" I ask Mya, gesturing for her to lead the way to the front door.

She rolls her eyes but walks in front of me, confidently striding into the foyer.

"Hi, Eve," Mya says, moving quickly to shut the front door. She grabs the woman's arm and pulls her into the living room. "Sit," she commands, pointing at an overstuffed sofa. "We want to talk to you."

Millie sits down, her eyes flicking nervously between the two of us. I know it's her. She licks her lips and twists her hands together in front of her. Her nerves are too obvious, something that Eve would never have allowed to show through.

"Is something wrong?" she says. "Why are you here? I did what you wanted earlier. I helped Mya with the drop. What are you doing here?"

"You were supposed to be here for me to get into the safe," Mya says, pulling a chair over to sit down in front of Millie.

I stand, watching, enjoying how this is playing out.

"Where were you?" Mya asks.

"Out. I went shopping."

"You don't have any bags."

Mya's fast for once.

Millie blushes, something I never once saw Eve do. "I didn't see anything I liked."

"Not even with your sister's credit card ready for you to spend as much money as you wanted?"

Both women look up at me when I speak. Mya may not have been on the same page with me when we got here, but she sees it now, and she smirks. Millie pales.

Again, not something Eve would ever do.

Eve may have been angry at us for having the upper hand, but she never blushed. She never ran her mouth; she never pushed us. She knew full well that the only way she was going to walk away from her meetings with us was to keep her mouth shut and do what we told her to do.

"My sister is gone," Millie tells us, crossing her arms. "She left town after getting out of prison, and I have no idea where she is."

"Right." I walk over to her. Dropping down on the sofa next to her, I throw my arm around her shoulders, ignoring how she tries to pull away from me and how Mya's eyes narrow at the sight. "She left town. Only she didn't, did she? Because she's you. *Millie*. Not Eve."

"You're insane." She tries to stand up, but I grab her shoulder, forcing her to sit back down.

"Millie, come clean. You can't keep pretending forever." I'm not used to people refusing to do what I want, and my patience is wearing thin. "You got rid of Eve somehow. How? Did she feel bad for framing you, so she let you move into her house and take over her life? Maybe you thought you were getting the good end of the deal because you had no idea what she was actually up to. Is that what happened?"

Millie shakes her head, her blonde hair fanning out around her. "No, I don't know what you're talking about. I'm Eve! Millie got out of prison and left town!"

"Or did you kill her?" My voice is so low that I don't think Mya hears me, but Millie does.

She freezes and slowly looks at me, her eyes wide. Her breathing is shallow, erratic. I can smell the fear wafting off her. I glance up at Mya, pleased to see the smile spreading across her face.

Mya may not have seen the truth about this woman being Millie at first, but it's clear she does now.

"You did kill her!" A surprised Mya scoots closer, leaning so far forward that she's perched on the edge of the chair. "You took over your sister's life."

For a moment I think Millie is going to argue with her. I'm convinced she's going to continue to fight this as long as she can. But her shoulders suddenly slump forward, and she drops her head into her hands.

"How did you know?" Her voice is low, quiet. She obviously wants to talk about this, but she doesn't want to admit it. "How could you tell?"

"You're not nearly as mean as your sister." I stand up and stretch. The gun pressing into the small of my back hurts a little bit. "You think that you're tough because you survived prison, but your sister had her husband murdered and framed you. Of course we knew you weren't her."

"So then where is she?" Mya sounds excited. Her eyes are wide, her lips parted. She obviously can't wait to hear what Millie is going to say. "Did she leave town?"

Mya is still one step behind me and thinks Eve might still be alive, but I've already figured out the truth.

For a moment, nobody moves; then Millie looks up at me. It's clear she's looking for guidance, looking for some sign I could give her to tell her what to do. When I don't react, she finally sighs. "She's gone."

"You killed her." A smile curls the corners of my lips. "You killed your twin and thought you were going to live the perfect life, didn't you? Amazing." This is too rich.

When we blackmailed Eve and told her she had to help us or we were going to turn her over to the police, I thought there was going to be an expiration date on the work we did together, but not because she was going to die. I thought for sure she would run or try to turn on us, and we would have to kill her.

This is too rich.

Money talks, and although Eve paid for silence, we were able to buy the information we wanted about the hitman she hired to kill Joe. From there, it was a simple task of sitting down with her and telling her we were more than happy to turn her over to the police if she refused to help us.

She was so afraid when we approached her, so nervous that we were going to force her to participate in illegal activities. Then I reminded her she'd already killed her husband. It wasn't like she could get much more illegal than that. Eve was so terrified, wanted so badly to run, but we explained to her what she probably already knew—that the only place she'd be going if she turned her back on us was to prison.

Her sister stares at me now, the same look of defiance on her face that Eve wore when we told her what she was going to be doing for us. She hated us for installing that safe in her bedroom, hated us for making her store things here for us.

But she didn't have a choice. She thought she was evil, she thought she was going to get away with having her husband killed and framing her sister for it, but what she didn't know was that there are more evil people in the world than her.

Like us.

And like her twin, apparently.

The three of us are silent, each of us lost in our own thoughts. I have no idea what Millie and Mya are thinking, but I'm the one who matters, and I already know what we're going to do.

Millie is exactly who we need. Sure, we're going to have to keep a tight leash on her to make sure she doesn't do something risky, but I'm ready for that, and Mya is, too. Now that she believes what I was saying about Millie not being Eve, Mya will be all over it. She'll make sure Millie doesn't get away; she'll make sure she doesn't do anything that will draw attention to us.

"What do you want from me? Are you going to call the police?" Millie lifts her chin a little bit and stares at me, like that's enough to scare me off or make me change my mind about what I want from this woman.

Nothing is going to make me change my mind. Gifts like Millie don't fall in your lap every single day, and I've learned not to turn my back on them when they do.

"You're going to take over for Eve," I tell her, enjoying how her face falls when she grasps what I'm saying. "We have a good thing here. We enjoyed working with your sister, and there's no way in hell we want to stop that, do you understand? You can have Eve's life, Millie, like you obviously wanted, but that means you get all of it."

She blinks at me. "I won't do it."

"You murdered Eve." Mya grins at Millie, then glances at me for approval. When I nod, she continues, "You killed your sister and dumped her body somewhere." She laughs; the sound is low and wry.

"Millie, think about it. Do you think the police would be willing to look the other way if we told them Eve was missing? Do you really think the detectives would miss out on an opportunity to send you back to jail?" I'm enjoying this more than I probably should.

Millie's breathing fast, releasing tiny little gasps of air that don't fill her lungs up completely. She keeps looking between the two of us, and I'm sure she's going to argue, sure she's going to make a run for it. Something.

But she looks me dead in the eyes, and what she says next thrills me.

25

MILLIE

SUNDAY

I wake up, roll over in bed and stretch, letting my fingers slide over the silk sheets that are softer than anything I've ever felt in my life. For a moment, I forget where I am. I somehow managed to forget everything that happened yesterday, the stress I felt, how terrified I was.

And then it hits me, slamming into me so hard that it forces me to sit up and grab my chest. Gasping for air, I look around the room, terrified that Gareth or Mya are in here with me. Terrified they're watching me from the chair in the corner of the room, or in the middle of opening the safe to drop something off, but I relax when I see it's just me.

I'm alone, and the only sound I hear is the ticking of Eve's watch on the bedside table. It's a Cartier, ostentatious and over the top—nothing I ever would have picked for myself—but I wear it every day in the hopes that I'll be able to keep fooling everyone into thinking I'm Eve.

Except the moment I let my guard down, the two most dangerous people in my world worked out exactly who I am.

With a groan, I reach over to the bedside table and grab the glass of water, as well as the two pain pills I left out the night before. My head pounds. It's not like I drank an entire bottle of wine last night to make it hurt this bad. This headache isn't from drinking, it isn't from staying out all night partying, and it certainly isn't from sitting up all night with a good book.

The only reason my head pounds is because I can't believe what I said to Gareth last night.

He stood there in front of me, looking more confident than anyone I've ever seen in my life, and told me exactly what I was going to do for him and Mya.

And I agreed to it.

I agreed, even though I saw the look of excitement in his eyes as he told me. It thrilled him that I agreed outright rather than try to get out of whatever little arrangement he had with my sister. But I didn't have a choice.

"God, what have I done?"

I rub my eyes, pressing down hard enough on my eyelids until explosions of light fill my vision. It hurts and feels good at the same time, and I don't stop until I worry I'm going to pass out. Dropping my hands, I get out of bed, wrap a robe around myself, and walk downstairs.

The house is deathly silent. When I get into the kitchen and push open a window, I can't even hear any birds outside. The day is dreary, damp, gray, and somehow I'm supposed to enjoy it.

That's what Gareth said last night with a laugh that made my stomach cramp. He said to enjoy my day off, then told me to get ready, because I'd be working hard for him on Monday.

I make some coffee and carry it to the table, where I sit

down and try to think through my options. I could run, of course. I have no idea how far I would get before someone found me, but Eve's passport is sitting upstairs, and nobody would look twice at the picture if I was leaving the country.

Running isn't something that I ever thought I'd stoop to, though. This house, the money Eve has—almost everything in her life is perfect, and I don't want to give that up. At the same time, I'm not sure how I can have the dream house and life and still deal with Gareth and Mya on a regular basis.

I told them last night I would work for them because I didn't think I had much of a choice. What was I going to do, tell him no? The man terrifies me, not only because of the things he has me do and the stuff he has stashed upstairs, but also because of the way he looks at me. I can't shake the feeling that he can read my mind and is pleased to discover it's the same as his.

"You messed up, Millie," I say, dropping my head into my hands. "How in the world are you going to get out of this one?"

Time slips by as I think of ways to change my situation. I desperately cling to each new idea as it comes to me before I discard it for the next one that might be a better solution to my problems.

"You can't run," I say to myself as I get up and walk to the refrigerator. "As much as you'd like to, where would you go? And how in the world could you guarantee that they wouldn't call the cops as soon as they figured it out?"

Grabbing some eggs from the fridge, I turn and put them by the stove and walk over to the sink, ready to pull a pan from the dish drainer. That's when I see something outside the window.

Leaving the pan for the moment, I twitch the curtains back. My stomach drops instantly. A black SUV turns slowly into the cul-de-sac, then pauses at the bottom of my driveway before turning and driving back out. There's no way it's a neighbor. That much is clear right away.

It's Mya or Gareth or one of the thugs they work with, and they're here to intimidate me. Dropping the curtain like it burned me, I step back from the window.

Running won't work. I'm sure that drive-by was just a show to prove to me they're watching everything I do. Mya and Gareth wouldn't waste their time coming by the house unless they wanted to make a point, and they made it.

"Okay, so they're watching you," I say, wiping my hands on the kitchen towel before angrily grabbing the pan from the drainer. "They have eyes on you, so leaving isn't exactly something you can do. But then what's the plan? You can't continue to live this life and do whatever it is they want you to do for them. That's not sustainable."

I think as I cook, and soon the kitchen smells amazing. There's half a loaf of bread I picked up at the bakery the other morning. I use it to make some French toast, soaking the end product in maple syrup. I refill my coffee cup and sit back down. Maybe, with a bit of food in me, I'll be able to think through what's going on.

Maybe, after I've had something to eat and taken a shower, I'll be able to calm down. Right now, it's almost impossible to even consider the idea, not when everything in my life is falling apart.

But I'm going to take care of this.

I'll take care of everything.

I grab my phone and flip through the news like I do every morning, making sure nothing about my release from prison has been mentioned. I thought I was doing such a great job pretending to be Eve with Mya and Gareth, but they saw right through me.

Who knows who else will be able to tell that I'm not Eve?

Alex. The thought of the officer hits me hard. So far, I've been able to keep our interactions to a minimum and avoided him the best I can, but that's not going to last forever. It's Sunday, and we have a standing date on Wednesdays, so it's only a matter of time before the two of us are stuck together.

Could I call off the date?

I could, but I'm not going to right now. The last thing I need is for Alex to become suspicious of me and think that I'm not Eve. That might happen when we spend time together, of course, but I get the impression that Eve never missed her date with Alex. Skipping out on him this Wednesday might put my mind at ease for a short period of time, but I have a very strong feeling it would come back to haunt me later.

No, I have to keep my date with Alex. For the time being, I'm going to do whatever Mya and Gareth ask of me. Then I know what I have to do.

I need to kill them both.

26

MILLIE

MONDAY

Mya's enjoying this too much.

"No, I want the truth. Where did you bury her?"

It's the second time she's asked the question, and just like the first time, I grit my teeth and turn away from her. She has to know I'm not going to cause a scene, not in the middle of Blue Sky restaurant, but that doesn't mean I can stop her talking about this.

What if someone were to overhear her? What if the waitress lingers too long and picks up on what she's saying, or the nosy man behind us who keeps glancing at us over the top of the paper he's reading finally understands her?

"Would you please stop bringing that up?" I'm frustrated, and I shouldn't let that show, because it's only going to push her to continue, but I can't help it. I need to get this woman to shut up, and it's not like I can yell at her right here in the restaurant.

That's why she wanted to meet here, I'm sure of it.

"Okay, but I'm going to find out eventually, understood?" She jabs her fork at me, a piece of lettuce still hanging from the tines. "Just so we're clear, lunch on Monday is mandatory. We also get our nails done every Thursday together, which gives me time to make sure you haven't messed up earlier in the week. And on the weekends I'll swing by to give you whatever other information you need for your drops. Got it?"

I nod, feeling numb. I have a chicken pesto wrap in front of me, but I've barely touched it. The thought of eating right now makes me want to throw up.

"You know," I say, swallowing hard before I continue, "I thought you and Eve were best friends."

This makes her laugh, and now a few new diners turn and look at us. When she stops laughing, she wipes her eyes, then reaches across the table to pat my hand.

Her skin is smooth and soft. I fight off the wave of revulsion washing over me when she touches me.

"No, no, not best friends," she says, taking a sip of her tea. "You can think of me more as her handler, but the last thing Gareth and I wanted was for people to get suspicious about our relationship. It worked, huh? Best friends. That's rich."

I stare at her. She's gorgeous, absolutely stunning, with thick hair that falls down her back and lips that are always boasting a coat of bright-red lipstick. But now that I know her better, I realize how evil she is. It's terrifying to think that a dark and dangerous personality could live right below the surface of someone and you would never know.

Like it did with Eve.

Like it does with me.

Shaking my head to clear the thought, I lean forward, not because I want to get closer to her, but because I want to keep everyone else from hearing what I'm about to say next. "What do I need to do?"

She grins and pushes her plate out of the way, her salad mostly gone. When the waitress walks over to pick it up, Mya doesn't acknowledge her. "You remember the two men we met in the woods?"

I nod. My blank expression is a mask.

"Good. Well, you're going to meet with them and pick up some cash."

"We just dropped off cash," I point out. "Why do I need to pick it back up?"

She doesn't blink. "Because, Eve, that cash was an advance. A loan. They're paying it back, with interest."

I ignore the fact that she called me by my sister's name. The only time she or Gareth called me Millie was when we were in the privacy of my house, and I have a good feeling I'm always going to be Eve to them out in public.

"What did they do to get enough money to pay it back that quickly?" It's the wrong thing to ask, I'm sure, but the words are out of my mouth before I can stop them.

"That is not something for you to worry about, little gopher. That's all you are in this, Eve, our gopher. We tell you where to go and what to do, and you do it. Got it?"

I nod, and she pushes a small slip of paper across the table to me. Without looking at it, I already know what it is.

Instructions on where to go, whom to meet. All of the instructions I need not to mess up royally will be written on this little slip of paper, but I don't want to touch it.

"Good girl. Pick up the tab, would you?"

Before I realize what she said, she stands up and walks out of the restaurant. More than a few patrons turn to watch her as she goes, and I don't blame them.

Mya is gorgeous. But there are few people I've met who are more evil than the woman who just had lunch with me.

One of them is my sister, and she's dead and buried. I'm another, which is something Mya would never guess about me.

I pick up the little slip of paper and open it, smoothing it out on the table. I'm supposed to meet the guys at two this afternoon, downtown, right outside McFarlan's bakery. The thought of doing business with two dangerous-looking men out in the open makes me nervous.

But I'll do it. If this is the game Mya and Gareth want to play with me, I'll play it with them. For now.

I didn't work hard to get out of prison only to end up in another one, with them as my jailers. No, I can't do this. I can't play their game, no matter what the threat. I have other plans.

Crumpling the paper in my palm, I throw more than enough cash down on the table and head for the door. I'm going to be a little bit early to the meeting spot, but I don't have enough time to go home. Once I get this cash, I'll drop it off in my safe. After, I'll have to figure out what I'm going to do.

As I see it, only one of us can come out on top, and I refuse for it to not be me.

That thought runs through my mind as I hurry out the door of Blue Sky and run straight into someone unexpected.

27

MILLIE

MONDAY

"Where's the fire?" Alex's easy grin catches me off guard more than slamming straight into him. His hands are on my arms, his grip gentle, as he helps me keep my balance. I feel his body warmth radiating off him.

"Alex, hey," I say, ignoring his question and smiling up at him. "I didn't see you there."

This is weird, right? It seems bizarre to me that I'd run into him again so soon. This is the second time in a week. Sure, this is a small town, but that doesn't mean I should keep running into Alex. If he weren't a cop and hopefully a great guy, I'd honestly be worried he is following me.

Sometimes, the truth is weird, and I think we're just two people who bump into each other.

"Obviously," he says. "Although, I have to admit, Eve, seeing you when I don't expect to is always a pleasure."

There's that smile again, the one that somehow managed to melt my sister's icy heart. She was evil through and through, but this man managed to get through to her, managed to get her to care for him.

It's terrible, but I'm going to have to break it off. Until I deal with Gareth and Mya, it's not safe for me to date a cop.

"I was heading out for a hair appointment," I lie, grabbing the ends of my strands and glancing at them. "I have more split ends than I've had in my entire life, and if I don't take care of them soon, then you're going to be dating someone bald."

He still holds on to me. It's difficult to extricate myself from his grip, but I do, then sidestep around him on the sidewalk.

The last thing I need is for Mya to be watching this inter-action. A quick glance around the parking lot reassures me, and I relax—but only a little bit. I don't see her car, but that doesn't mean she's really gone. She could be here, watching, wanting to know what I'm going to do or say, making sure I'm not going to do something stupid.

"Your hair looks great. And I wouldn't care if you were bald." Alex reaches for the door to Blue Sky and swings it open. "I'm grabbing something to-go, and then I have to head back to the office to work on reports." He adjusts his duty belt, the gun and walkie that look heavy on his hips.

"You are the sweetest," I tell him, taking another step back from him. "Are we still on for Wednesday?"

I want him to say no. I want him to cancel because then I won't have to worry about sitting down across from this man and talking to him. The less time I spend with him, the less likely it is that he'll figure out I'm not Eve.

"Are you kidding me? I work my entire schedule around Wednesday. Seven o'clock, Lorenzo's. I'll see you there." With that, he's gone, and I'm left alone on the sidewalk, my mind spinning.

First of all, I'm glad to know where I'm going to be meeting this man. Lorenzo's isn't in town, it's two towns over, so no matter how reckless Eve was in meeting up with Alex every week, at least she wasn't having dinner with him downtown where Mya or Gareth could see her.

Secondly, I don't see a way out of this right now, but dealing with Alex isn't my top priority.

I glance at my watch and groan when I see the time. It's not so late that I'm going to have to run to make it to the drop in time, where I agreed to grab the cash from the men in the woods, but I do need to hurry. So I set off down the sidewalk, looking over my shoulder at Blue Sky one more time.

As I walk, I try to come up with a plan, but I can't seem to hold on to any thought for long enough to figure out what to do. Alex seems like a nice guy, and in another life, maybe...

But not this one.

I walk around a group of teenagers who definitely don't look old enough to be out of school today, and make my way to the bench. I sit down, then scoot over to sit on the side in the shade.

1:55 pm.

Exhaling, I look around for the men I'm supposed to meet.

I see nobody.

At 1:59 pm I check my watch again, nervous that I may have missed them. It's entirely possible that I'm on the wrong bench or that they chose to go to a different one or something. But Mya wouldn't send me on an errand unless all the pieces were in order. I don't know why I think that about her, but I get the feeling she doesn't make mistakes.

2:01 pm.

I shift on the bench, looking down the sidewalk, hoping I

won't see Alex walking toward me. The last thing I need is for him to see me here and not at the hair salon, where I told him I'd be.

2:05 pm.

My phone vibrates, and I yank it from my purse. My heart sinks when I see the message from Mya.

I'm at your house. You'd better not be running.

I feel claustrophobic. My chest tightens, and my hands tremble as I respond to her.

They haven't shown yet. I'm waiting.

I flip my phone over and over in my hand and look around again, putting my arm on the bench next to me so I can twist around and look over my shoulder. I have no clue where these guys are, but the last thing I need is for Mya to think I'm trying to leave town. A cold sweat breaks out on my brow when I think about her and Gareth coming to find me because they thought I stole their money.

Millie, don't do anything stupid, I warn myself.

"Oh, God," I mutter, tapping the back of the phone nervously while trying to think about what to do next. "Oh, shit. What do I do?"

2:10 pm.

"Eve."

A man drops down onto the bench next to me and grins, looking like someone who didn't make me wait ten minutes. I feel rage bubbling up inside me.

"You're late," I snap at him, surprising even myself at my boldness. "Do you have the money?"

His smile disappears. "Jesus, you don't have to be a bitch about it."

He runs a hand through his hair to push it back from his face, stares at me, then opens his jacket and reaches inside. When he pulls out a wad of money, I shake my head.

I remember how much Mya took from the safe on Saturday, and there's no way this is everything.

"That's not it," I tell him. I remember what Gareth and Mya told me to say. "And there's interest, too."

The man chuckles and shakes his head. He looks surprised about what I'm saying to him. I am too, if I'm honest.

I keep my jaw set the way I saw Eve do a million times when we were growing up, but my palms are sweaty, and I feel a trickle run down my back.

"You're good. I wondered, because you looked scared to death on Saturday." Raising his hand, he gestures for someone to come.

The second man appears, this time carrying one of the backpacks Mya and I gave him.

"You're smart not to try to take advantage of Gareth," I tell him, standing up and snatching the backpack from him.

It's heavy, but I still open it and glance inside, trying to keep my expression even. There's more money in here than I've ever seen in my life—rolls and rolls of bills, with rubber bands tied around them to keep them together.

"Next time, don't be late," I warn them.

Before either one of them can respond, I turn and stalk down the sidewalk. I feel self-conscious, but I need to keep moving.

If I stop, I might fall over. If I stop, then the full reality of what I did will hit me. If that happens, I'm not sure what I'm going to do.

As soon as I'm sitting in the car with the AC cranked and blowing in my face, I grab my phone and respond to Mya.

I have it. On my way.

There. She was upset before, and I get that, but she can't possibly be mad at me now. I'm doing everything she and Gareth wanted me to do, and I'm doing it without complaining.

When I'm halfway out of the parking space, my phone buzzes. I stop and grab it, thumbing the screen to read the message before I move the car another inch.

You passed. Can't wait to tell you what you're doing next.

28

MYA

TUESDAY

Millie's late.

I thought we made it clear to her how this was going to go and that she didn't have a choice in the matter. I was sure we made it clear how she would be keeping up her sister's end of the deal with us, but the fact that she isn't here yet makes me a little nervous.

Craning my neck, I look around the restaurant. I'm not the only person sitting by myself, which means that nobody is paying attention to me here. That's one of the reasons why I love having meetings at Blue Sky. If it were odd for anyone to sit alone in a place like this, then I'd stand out.

But I'm just one more person waiting for someone to show up, and because of that, people's eyes skim right over me. It's the ideal scenario, and it gives me the opportunity to listen in on conversations. It gives me the chance to think more about recruiting other people to work for me and Gareth.

Finding Eve and getting her in our pocket right away was a surprise. Neither one of us thought it would be that easy to get help to distribute our drugs, but Eve took the pressure off us, which means we don't have to worry as much about someone tying us to the business.

It's amazing.

Eve fell into our lap. I remember seeing her in a bar years after her husband's murder trial. I remember how her face lit up when I sat down next to her and offered to buy her a drink. Clearly nobody wanted to be friends with someone so lonely, and with so much baggage. In the beginning, I thought she could be a hit. Gareth and I were always on the lookout for easy ways to make money, and what was easier than a friendless widow?

I found out pretty quickly that Eve wasn't as innocent as she was claiming to be. It was something she said, something about Joe finally being gone that twigged it. All it took then was for Gareth to make a few phone calls, make a few threats, and we knew all we needed to know.

We knew she paid someone to kill her husband. How she set it up so that Millie would take the fall. Eve was strong, but Millie might be stronger. Millie was in prison, and now she killed her sister. It's obvious that she's cunning and smart and willing to do whatever it takes to keep herself out of trouble and out of jail.

We have the same goals in that regard.

A cool breeze cuts across the restaurant when someone opens the door. Millie scoots across the space, her eyes scanning the room as though she isn't sure exactly whom she's going to be meeting. I raise my hand in annoyance to get her attention.

"Mya, hi." She drops into the chair across from me and

takes a sip of the iced tea I ordered for her. "Sorry about being a bit late."

"That seems to be a problem with you recently," I snap, making a show of checking my watch. I have an appointment this afternoon, one I can't miss. Luckily, my coat is in the car, and I can throw it on over what I have on. Nobody will blink an eye at my attire when I show up.

"It won't happen again," she says.

It's a lie. I can tell just by looking at Millie. She's having trouble making eye contact. I should be worried about what's going on with her on a personal level, but I don't care. The only reason I enquire about what's happening with her is because I can't afford for her to mess this up.

"You have another drop to make today," I tell her. "The bag is in my car. Remember where you met Gareth in the park?"

"By the river."

I nod. "Same place. Five o'clock. Don't be late, Eve, or Gareth will have to get involved. Trust me, that won't end up good for you. It's best if you figure out now how to make sure you'll be on time."

Gareth and I agreed to call her Eve in public in case anyone is eavesdropping. Now that I know the truth, that she's Millie and not Eve, I like to rub it in. I like to make sure she remembers that she can't hide from us.

I watch her reaction, wait to see what she's going to say next. Gareth and I made it clear to her how this was going to go, but Millie's smart. She looks like she's thinking. Like maybe she thinks she has a way out of this.

No, surely not. We have her locked down. That's the one thing Gareth and I made sure of with Eve, and we worked hard to keep her from running. The last thing we wanted was for Eve to get any ideas about leaving us or think about turning us over to the police. That's why the safe is at her house.

That's also why we made her take the picture of it on her phone, as proof that she knew it was there. Gareth made her take the shot so she would always have it as a reminder of who she works with. Plus, we had the dirt on her over her hit on Joe. And now that Millie admitted to killing her twin, there's no way in hell she's going to get out of this arrangement.

We had Eve under our thumb, and now we have Millie. She might hate herself, might hate me, might daydream about getting out of this, but there's no way she can.

We're secure, but there's a look on Millie's face that makes me nervous.

"How much longer?" She leans forward and stares at me.

Over the top of her head, I see the waitress start to walk over to us, but I wave her away.

"How much longer, Mya? I want out."

I can't believe she's trying to start this with me right now. How many times did I have to remind her sister that she didn't have a choice but to work with us? More than I can count.

I don't want to go through the same thing with Millie.

I stare at her, trying to decide the best way for me to handle this. I can only imagine what Gareth would say, but he's not here, and I want to take care of this on my own. Besides, we have a good thing going with Millie, and I have no doubts that I can control her.

"You remember what we talked about, right? You know there's no way in hell we're letting you walk away from this," I tell her. "There's no end to this unless Gareth and I say there is."

She's silent. The sounds of the restaurant swell in the

silence between us. People are talking, clinking silverware, laughing.

She doesn't move.

"I know that," she tells me, "but I didn't agree to this. My sister did." Her cheeks are flushed. I think she's gearing up to argue with me, but I'm not interested in hearing it.

"No." It's not an option, and she knows it. I have no idea what's gotten into her that she thinks this is a conversation I'm willing to have with her. "No. You need to stop that way of thinking. You belong to us. You work for us. I don't care what you think you want. I promise you that our agreement is a hell of a lot better than going to prison. A hell you should know well, right? Are you willing to risk going back to prison? You killed someone for this life."

My voice is so low that she's the only one who can hear what I'm saying. Still, I want to push my point, want to make sure she sees how serious I am.

"Don't think for a second that we're not willing to put you next to Eve." I'm hissing the words at her. "You want to push this? Push it. But you won't walk out of it in one piece. I will."

There's a flash of emotion on her face, but it's gone as fast as it came. I stare at her, trying to work out what she's thinking, trying to figure out how I can get inside her head and make her see that she doesn't have a choice in this matter.

She plays by our rules, or she won't be playing any games at all.

"You need to get your head on straight," I tell her. "Come on." Angrily, I pull cash from my wallet and throw it on the table. It's more than enough to not only cover our drinks but also keep the waitress happy.

Millie stands up, too slowly, but she follows me to the door.

Outside, I walk straight to my car, push the button on my remote to unlock the trunk, then grab a bag for her. She hesitates when I hold it out to her, but finally takes it, her jaw tight, her eyes locked on somewhere beyond me.

"Put the money in the safe when you get home," I tell her. "Gareth and I aren't planning on stopping by to check it, but that shouldn't be a problem, should it? You're a big girl, and you know how to do what's best for you."

She doesn't respond. Her jaw is still tight, her cheeks flushed.

"Don't mess this up. You know what will happen to you if you try to cross us. The last thing you want is to go to prison for killing your sister."

Her mouth opens, but then she snaps it shut.

"What were you going to say?"

I'm teasing her, provoking her. It's insane, and I should stop, but right now I can't. Millie has to get this through her head. She has to understand that there isn't an out for her. This is her life, the one she agreed to, and it's a hell of a lot better than being locked up for the rest of her natural life.

There's no way that she'd be willing to give up Eve's life just to go back to prison. I've never been there, personally, but I know plenty of people who have. Who gives a shit if Millie has to do some work for us from time to time?

She's not in prison. She could be. I could make it happen.

"I'll do the drop today," she says, adjusting her gaze so she's staring right at me. "Happy?"

"Thrilled." I slam the trunk and brush past her to get in my car. The white of my coat on the back seat catches my eye. I glance at it once, glad I thought to bring it with me for my next meeting.

"Before you think about doing something foolish, Eve, remember the tracker." I throw this little tidbit over my shoulder at her, glancing at her to catch the expression on her face.

Panic. Rage. It's a gorgeous mixture, and it tells me that we have her.

Millie watches as I pull out of the parking space. I have a tiny nagging thought in the back of my mind that she's going to do something she shouldn't, but I shake my head to clear it. She won't. Not after our talk.

She's ours.

Gareth and I made sure of that.

By the time I pull out of the parking lot, I see she's in her car, backing out of the space. I can't see her face from here, but I don't need to. She's angry.

Be angry, Millie. You killed your sister and took over her life. Now you have to pay for that.

29

MILLIE

TUESDAY

It's still warm enough during the day that I can get away with not wearing long sleeves, but the late afternoon is a different story. I stamp my feet and rub my hands together while I wait by the river for whomever I'm supposed to meet for the drop.

It doesn't help any that I'm tucked away in the woods, that I'm standing by the river, or that the breeze blowing off the water is chilly, but I'm glad I put on a coat before I left the house.

The bag Mya gave me sits at my feet. I want to throw it into the water and walk away from this. The thought crosses my mind more than once, but I'm not sure how I would escape if I did that. Mya said that she and Gareth weren't coming by tonight to make sure I have all the money. I could run.

But then I think about what Mya said to me in the Blue Sky parking lot.

A tracker.

But where? The first thing I did after meeting with her was head straight home and go online to look up what kind of trackers are in use. I followed instructions and did a clean reset of my phone after and cleared everything out—not that there was much to clear in the first place. I wrote down Mya's and Gareth's numbers so I wouldn't accidentally screen their calls.

That was supposed to take care of any trackers on my phone, but now I'm wondering about my car. They could have a bug in it, could have something that tells them exactly where I am, and that thought gives me chills. Maybe I should sell the car. Maybe, if I wait until the right time, I can sell it, buy another one straight away, and then leave town.

It's clear what I have to do if I'm going to make it out of this in one piece.

When I close my eyes, I see Mya's face outside Blue Sky— twisted with anger, but there was also a hint of glee that tells me she's confident she's won. She looked nice, ready to go on a date or to work. Her high heels clicked on the ground as we walked across the parking lot. Her hair and makeup were flawless.

Wherever she was going, she was in a rush.

"Are you the drop?" A woman's voice surprises me, and I whip around, my heart picking up the pace. Eyeballing her, I try to regain my composure; then I nod.

"Do you have the cash?"

The woman looks normal. She has on running gear like she is out for a predinner jog; her high ponytail sways from side to side when she nods. Shrugging off her backpack, she then unzips it and holds it out for me to look inside.

I see what I came for.

"Great. Give it to me."

I pick up my bag and reach inside to pull out the package of pills. They're mixed together, all colors and shapes, wrapped tightly with Saran Wrap. I have no idea what kind of pills they are or where they come from, but I keep telling myself that's not my problem.

What, like knowing where Gareth and Mya get their illegal pills is going to help me out? I think not.

The woman grins as she presses money into my hand and takes the pills.

"Have a good evening."

I watch her zip them in her backpack, shoulder the bag, clip it around her waist, then run back up the trail.

This entire time I haven't moved. My heart is going so fast, I feel like I'm going to pass out. How many meetings have I had? Two? Three?

I'm not sure, but they're wearing on me. I can't understand how Eve did this, day in and day out. Sure, her life looked amazing, and she definitely had the money to do whatever she wanted in her free time, but it's only been a few weeks since I got out of prison, and I'm not sure I can keep this pace up.

The adrenaline coursing through my body makes me feel energetic. I want to burn off the energy, but instead I wait a few minutes to make sure the woman is gone, then walk up the path. It's going to take me a few minutes to get to my car. I was nervous about parking too close to the drop point in case someone saw me and wanted to know what I'm doing.

I'm halfway across the parking lot to my car when someone calls my name.

Well, my sister's name.

"Eve! Wait up!"

The voice makes me stiffen, and I turn slowly, almost afraid to see who might be coming up behind me. I'm not entirely sure that I want to know who is hunting me down, not after I sold a bunch of drugs to someone and have rolls of cash in my backpack.

Besides, the only friends of my sister I've met are Gareth, Mya, and Alex, and it's not like I would consider them friends.

"Hey, Eve. What are you doing here so late?" The woman who stops in front of me looks excited to see me. When I don't immediately answer, she reaches out and pats my arm. "I haven't seen you in years and almost wasn't even sure it was you! You know, I heard about your twin getting out of prison, and I thought for a moment..." Her voice trails off.

I clear my throat. "You thought I was Millie? Not a chance." I force a chuckle. "Sorry I didn't see you at first. I was deep in my own thoughts."

"No problem. I was a little surprised after you told me you didn't need anyone to clean your house for you any longer. It's so big, and you're there all alone now, but you must have things under control." She chuckles. "It's not like I did that much, I guess. You were always so neat and had things dusted and mopped before I even got there."

Eve fired her house cleaner? Of course, I'd guess she'd have to in case the woman got too suspicious about what was going on in the house.

I smile at her, doing my best to look natural.

Calm. Like I don't have anything to hide.

"You know how it is," I say, still smiling. "You were an incredible cleaner, but I needed to be alone. So I appreciate you understanding that."

"No problem. If you ever change your mind, you have my number, okay?"

I do not.

"Sure do, and thanks. I appreciate you stopping to chat." I

throw her another smile. "Gotta get home. Pilates bright and early in the morning."

"Yeah, don't let me keep you. It was good to see you. I'm glad you're doing okay. Have a great night, Eve!" She waves and backs up to give me space to get in my car.

As soon as I do, I lock the doors. It's not that I think this woman is going to try to get into the car and come home with me, but I'm realizing how little I know about people in this town.

I didn't know that Eve was selling drugs for someone. I certainly didn't know she was in a relationship with a cop. And now for a random person to recognize me and approach me? It makes me nervous. I'm terrified that someone who knew Eve while I was in prison will come up to me and want to talk longer than this woman did.

What if they figure out that I'm not Eve?

A fine sweat breaks out on my brow at the thought, and I drive slowly through the parking lot, making sure I'm not speeding or doing anything that might draw attention to me.

I just want to get home.

No, scratch that. I want to get out of here. Becoming Eve was a split-second decision I made after she slammed the door in my face. It made me realize that we would never connect or be able to co-exist. I'm beginning to think that it might have been a mistake.

I'm beginning to think that maybe I traded one prison for another.

I have to do something about Mya and Gareth. Killing them is the best plan I have right now, but I'm not sure if I can go through with it. I did that once—killed someone—and I have no idea if I can do it again.

But maybe I won't have a choice.

As I drive, something occurs to me. Gareth and Mya have all the power here. They know everything about me—about

Eve—and they're not afraid to use that information to keep me in line. To hurt me. To make it impossible for me to actually live the life I stole from my sister.

But maybe I can take it back. I have to get some information on Mya and Gareth. I have to learn who they are, what they do, and what I can do to stop them, and then maybe I'll be able to live the life I deserve.

I keep thinking about killing them, but maybe I don't have to go that far. Maybe, in order to live the life I always wanted, I can keep my hands clean.

I'm going to have to ruin theirs.

30

MILLIE

WEDNESDAY

I'm nervous as I drive out of town to meet Alex. He's insistent that the two of us not miss our Wednesday date, and while I'm not sure that going out with him right now is the best option—not when I'm trying to think of a way to flee town without Mya or Gareth knowing—I'm pretty sure that I don't have a choice in the matter.

I absolutely have to break up with him. The drop I did yesterday made that clear to me.

But first I need to make sure that Alex isn't going to do something stupid, like show up at my house with flowers and a boom box a la *Say Anything*. He's no John Cusack, that's for sure, but if he did something like that and Mya or Gareth were around to witness it?

No.

I can't think about it. Just the thought of what could happen, of what the two of them might to do him, it's too much for me to wrap my mind around. I don't want to go down that path when I'm sure that coming back up it might prove too difficult.

The little Italian bistro where Eve and Alex meet once a week isn't very busy. I pull into one of the many empty parking spaces right in front of the restaurant, my head on a swivel as I look around for my date. It isn't until he raps on my window, making me jump, that I realize he's already here.

"Hey," I say, getting out of the car. I dressed up a little, not super fancy, because I didn't know what I'd need to wear. I'm glad to see that I look like I belong with Alex. He has on jeans and a jacket, but nothing over the top. I sigh with relief.

"You look lovely," he says, leaning in for a kiss.

I turn my head at the last second so it lands on my cheek. There's surprise on his face, but I smile and lean away from him.

"I'm sorry, I have this killer cold. My head feels like it's going to explode, and the last thing you need is to get it and then have to call in sick to work. I'm so glad to see you though."

"Oh, I'm sorry." He takes my hand, linking our fingers together.

It's more physical contact than I've had in years, and I almost pull away from him on instinct, but then I remind myself I have to do this.

He sincerely believes I'm Eve. I'm not sure how much longer I can keep up that charade, but I'm going to do my best.

The restaurant smells amazing, and I let Alex lead me to a table in the far corner. He pulls out the chair for me, and I sit, flapping out my napkin on my lap. Everything feels surreal, and I can't shake the thought that this is going to spell the end for me here. There's no way that he's going to believe that

I'm Eve, not when I'm sure he only has to look at me to tell I'm not her.

We look alike, sure, but it's pretty clear that Alex and Eve had an intimate relationship. I can't believe he doesn't realize that I'm not the woman he was dating.

Still, either the candlelight in the restaurant is working in my favor, or Alex isn't that bright. He sits across from me and sighs heavily.

"Tell me about your day," he says, reaching across the table to take my hand. He gives it a squeeze, and I have to resist the urge to pull it back so he can't touch me. "You always have the most interesting stories."

"Oh, you're too kind," I tell him, racking my brain for what to say. The best option for me right now is to lie and make something up, but I don't think that's going to work. "I haven't been feeling well, Alex. I'm sorry if I'm not the best company tonight."

He frowns. "You should have told me. I would have come over and made you chicken soup. There's no reason why we need to go out if you'd actually let me cook in your kitchen. I've never met anyone so concerned with keeping their house clean like you are."

"I get it. I'm simply terrible." I grin at him, hoping that I sound like Eve. "It's just that... I'm so careful in the kitchen, and I want to make sure it's always picked up so there isn't a mess to deal with later. Besides, don't you think that having someone make and bring you food after a long day of catching criminals and solving crimes is a nicer option?"

This makes him smile. He launches into some stories about his day; I listen but mostly tune him out. My brain is going a million miles a minute.

Alex is as big a problem as Mya and Gareth.

I never should have come here, but I didn't feel like I had a choice. If Alex thinks for one second that something is wrong, then it's likely he'll dig deeper to find out what's going on with me—and that's something I can't allow to happen.

"Oh, our food," he says, cutting off his own story and pointing at someone. "I love that we come here so often that they don't even have to take our order."

I look up in surprise when a waiter puts a plate of eggplant parmigiana in front of me. I'm sure it looks delicious to someone who likes eggplant, but I have to fight to keep from wrinkling my nose.

When I don't immediately grab my fork and dive in, Alex frowns. "You really don't feel good, do you? Normally you'd have half the plate gone by now."

"I'm so sorry, I don't." I push back the plate, not even wanting to see the eggplant parm in front of me. This was a terrible idea. It's one thing to accidentally run into Alex and talk to him for a few minutes, but to sit down across from each other and try to enjoy a meal?

I may be lucky, but there's no way that the light in here is so bad that he won't be able to tell I'm not Eve. Even with the flickering candles, even with the glass of wine he's currently drinking, he's going to figure out that something is up.

It's one thing to make drops in Eve's name. That's not dangerous. Well, it is, but only because the people I'm meeting with are dangerous. It's not dangerous because I'm worried about someone discovering who I am. Or who I'm not.

Dealing with Gareth and Mya is also dangerous, but this meal with Alex feels even worse. He's a police officer, for goodness' sake. He could arrest me right here if he suspected I'd done something wrong, and throw me in jail before I had a chance to even argue my case.

My mouth goes dry. I shouldn't drink, but I reach out and grab my glass anyway, taking three huge gulps before I finally can relax.

Alex is staring at me. He appears nervous, like he's not sure what's going on with me. Truth be told, I don't know myself. All I know is that I need to get out of here as quickly as possible.

"I don't feel good." I stand up and plant my hands on the table so I can get a better look at him. He's still staring at me like he's trying to figure me out.

Does he know?

Does he even have an inkling?

The wine I drank feels heavy in my stomach, and I turn from the table, suddenly needing air. I have to get out of here. I have to leave behind the soft Italian music, the smells of the food, the waiters with too-big grins.

But mostly I have to leave Alex.

If I don't, I have no idea what he's going to do.

"Eve, come back!" He stands and walks after me.

But I keep going, not daring to look back at him. I hit the restaurant door at a run, then stop outside, grabbing my thighs and sucking in gasps of air.

Alex catches up with me and rubs my back.

"Hey, are you okay?" His voice is softer, kinder. He is a good man, but that doesn't mean I need him in my life.

"I'm fine!" I snap the words at him, moving away so his arm drops uselessly to his side. Keeping my face angled away from the streetlamp, so it won't be easy for him to see who I am, I walk towards my car. "Just... let me go, Alex. I don't feel good."

He doesn't give up. He walks me to my car, holding the door open for me while I get in. "You don't seem yourself, Eve. Are you sure I can't help you?"

"No." I choke on the word but manage to get it out. "Just let me go. I need to go home."

After I back out and turn the car in the parking lot, I look back at him. He's still standing there where I left him, a dark look on his face.

He looks concerned.

No, that's not it.

He looks like he knows something that I don't.

But what secret could he have?

31

MYA

FRIDAY

Sometimes I have to remind myself that I really do love my job. Talking to people can be exhausting— listening to them talk about their problems can be even more so. I loved it in the beginning, when I got my job, but then Gareth and I had bigger plans.

We knew that we could work, could stash money away in accounts and IRAs and hope that nothing bad would happen to clear us out before we were able to retire or we could take matters in our own hands.

So we did.

I'm in the car, leaving work, and I call Gareth to check in on him. He's been busy recently, making sure that our pipelines are in place, that the people we're selling drugs to aren't making bad decisions that will come back to haunt us. I'm getting a little tired of not seeing him as often as I would like.

When he picks up, I can hear the stress in his voice, but

it's good to talk to him. "How's your day?" I ask, turning out of the parking lot and angling the car toward home. "You still have more work to do, or will you be able to make it home for dinner?"

"I'll be home." His tone shifts a little bit, becomes lighter. He's glad I'm calling and checking in on him, that much is obvious. Sure, we're both stressed, and yes, handling Millie suddenly feels like more of a full-time job than ever before, but it's all worth it.

Besides, she's not a good person. She's not kind, not thoughtful. She's a murderer, and she deserves whatever comes her way.

"Good. I thought I'd grill some steaks, crack open a bottle of wine, keep it simple. Just a nice evening at home with you."

"What's the occasion?"

"It was a good day." I haven't had to deal with Millie since Thursday. When I swung by her house yesterday to make sure all the money was in the safe where it was supposed to be, she was nervous, but she wasn't too much of a pain. "I think Millie was going through a rough patch there for a moment, but we have her nicely on board now. We might not have her tied up as much as we did Eve, but I have no doubt we'll be able to keep her."

"Good. We don't want to lose her. It wouldn't just be losing her, it would also be losing the safe."

I know.

"I don't think we need to worry about that." It's a short drive to the grocery store, and I pull in, park my car, relax back in my seat. "I'm gonna go because I'm at the store, but I'll see you soon, okay? Love you."

"I love you." He hangs up.

Before I get out of the car, I pull up the app on my phone that allows me to track Millie's car. This was my idea, just to make sure she wasn't going to run.

Gareth is more inclined to make threats and hope that the person will follow through on whatever they've been told to do. That's great, and it works, but I wanted to take it a step farther, so I did. I don't have a way to track Millie herself, but I can always see where her car is.

It takes a moment for the app to load, and I tap the side of the phone, growing impatient. I want to find out where she is, want to check in on her. I'm confident she's in our pocket now, but I still want to keep an eye on her.

I don't know why, but part of me can see her trying to run. I can see her making a break for it. That simply can't happen. As long as her car is in town, then I don't have to worry. I like to see her going from home to the store or to Pilates. I like knowing exactly where she is.

Finally the app loads, and I tap the screen, zooming in on the little car icon. Millie doesn't usually go places at night. She tends to stick close to home, making it easy for me to keep an eye on her.

But she's not at home.

That much is obvious immediately, but I still have to wait a moment for the streets to load on the app so I can tell exactly where she is.

The hospital.

"What in the world are you doing there?" Fear prickles the back of my mind. Millie is unpredictable, unlike Eve. We had Eve under control, and it's strange to have to go through that entire process again with her twin. I have no idea what Millie's doing at the hospital, but I don't like it.

I think back to when I saw her last. She seemed fine. Scattered. Not willing to keep working with me and Gareth, but physically she seemed fine. I guess the stress of what she's doing could be having an impact on her and is making her feel sick, but then why not go to a doctor? Why would she go to the hospital when there are plenty of doctors who I'm sure would love to see her and tell her that she needs to decrease the amount of stress in her life?

I swear as I run a hand through my hair, trying to think about what to do next. Normally, I wouldn't think about checking the app to see where Eve is, but dealing with her sister is an entirely different animal. I can't put my finger on what it is about her, but something doesn't feel right.

When I first put the tracker on Eve's car, I checked it all the time to make sure she wasn't going to try to leave town, but I haven't done that in years.

"Why in the world are you at the hospital?" If something is really wrong with her, then Gareth and I need to know about it.

And if she's running her mouth to someone, then I need to stop it.

There's a little voice in my head that whispers she might be following me, but I push it away.

Not a chance. She's not that smart.

32

MILLIE

SATURDAY

Following Mya is probably not a good idea, but if I'm going to kill her and Gareth, then I need to know what she does, where she goes, and how I can stop her from ruining my life. Chasing her around town is dangerous, but once I understand her routine, then I'll be in control.

I saw her car in the parking lot at the hospital yesterday when I drove by. I thought I'd be able to follow her, but she drove like a bat out of hell, and I lost her.

I missed her once, but I'm determined not to let that happen again, which is why I decided to head back today, on the off chance she'll be there.

I drive slowly now, taking my time as I try to find her. If she's not here, then I have no idea where she is. I loop through the last area of the parking lot, quickly scanning the rows of vehicles for her black BMW.

Nothing.

Drumming my fingers on the steering wheel, I swear, then turn around in an empty parking lot, ready to go back home.

This week has been a nightmare. From the meetings and drops I've done for Mya and Gareth, to learning that apparently Eve was loathed all around town—it all makes me want to crawl into bed and pretend this week never happened. So even though I want to find Mya, even though I want to see where she's going and what she's up to, I turn back to my house, wanting nothing more than to put on Eve's super-soft silk pajamas and have a glass of wine.

I thought that this plan was going to let me not only take over Eve's life but enjoy it to the fullest. I thought I'd be out on the town every night, drinking and dancing, meeting new friends—traveling even. I never once thought that I'd be exchanging one prison for another.

Never did I think that I'd have to stay in my house to avoid the people Eve made so mad; not once did I think I'd be working with drug dealers.

"Dammit!" I smack my palms hard against the steering wheel. I'm at a red light, and the driver in the car next to me inches forward a bit, his head turned to stare at me, but I don't care.

Angry tears run down my cheeks, and I wipe them away on the back of my hand, exhaling hard.

"This was not how any of this was supposed to go," I say, shaking my head. "I thought her life was perfect. I thought..." Well, it doesn't matter what I thought, does it?

And then it hits me.

Eve's life was hell, and now I'm living it.

Not only that, but she tried to tell me that when I killed her. She tried to tell me her life wasn't perfect, and I didn't listen to what she was saying.

Ignoring the anger in the pit of my stomach, I turn into

Eve's neighborhood, drive slowly past the manicured lawns and gorgeous front porches, and pull into my driveway. The garage door slides up smoothly, and I park the car inside, making sure to drop the door down behind me before I get out.

As I close the car door behind me, my phone rings. The number isn't saved, and at first, I don't want to answer it. Fear grips my chest when I try to imagine who might want to talk to me.

"Hello?" My voice shakes a little bit as I answer the phone. I don't want to know who's calling; don't want to speak to anyone who might be calling me, especially after meeting those two guys in the woods last week and again this week.

"Eve, hey, it's Alex." Relief pours through me when he speaks. I turn to lean against the car, my knees suddenly feeling weak. "What are you up to?"

"I just got home," I tell him, closing my eyes for a moment and trying to picture Eve's planner. I don't think I have anything planned with Alex for tonight, but then again, I got the impression that Eve wanted to keep Alex hidden from sight. Do we have plans? Am I supposed to be doing something with him right now?

"Oh, you did?" He sounds confused. "You told me forever ago that you didn't want neighbors gossiping about me coming over anymore, but there are some things I need to talk to you about in person. I hope you don't get mad, but I swung by before my shift started, and nobody was home. Well, that isn't true—there was an empty car in your driveway, but nobody answered the door when I rang the bell."

A chill runs up my spine, and I hurry into the house, locking the door to the garage. "What kind of car? I wasn't expecting anyone."

"Black BMW SUV."

I'm choking. I'm actually so convinced I'm going to choke

that I reach up and touch my neck. I run my fingers over my skin.

"Weird," I say, trying to keep my voice as even as possible. "I didn't know anyone would be coming by."

"Well, I'm sorry I missed you. How about I come by later this weekend? Maybe tomorrow I'll grab some dinner, and the two of us can talk."

"Do we need to talk?" The question is out of my mouth before I can stop it. "Is something wrong?"

"No, nothing at all. I just haven't seen you since Wednesday, and I'd like to."

If that's all it is, then it can wait. As nice as Alex seemed when I met him in the park, the last thing I want is for him to come over here, especially when there was someone at my house.

No, not *someone*. Mya. I'm confident who it was even though I wasn't here to see her car, wasn't here to see her go into my house. Slowly I walk toward the stairs. I run my hand over the banister, knowing full well that she was here a short time ago, and she probably went upstairs, probably helped herself to things in the safe.

"Oh, I know," I reply to Alex. "It's hard only seeing you on Wednesdays, but I really..." My voice trails off as I try to think about what else to say to get it through Alex's head that he can't come over here.

Not only that, but I need to get it through his head that this—whatever was going on between him and Eve—has to stop. There's no way it can continue, no way I can juggle dealing with him as well as Mya and Gareth.

I was already pretty sure of that when we went on our date on Wednesday, but now I'm convinced.

This has to end before he realizes I'm not Eve.

How in the world did my sister do it?

"You really what?" There's an edge to his words, and I

wince, even though they can't physically hurt me. "You know how I feel about you, Eve. I also told you that not seeing you very often is hard on me, and I want to get more serious with you. I wanted to tell you that on Wednesday, but you bailed out on me before I could bring it up."

Oh, God. The last thing I need is to get into a serious relationship with a police officer. No, it's more like *staying* in a serious relationship with a police officer.

Mya and Gareth can't know about Alex, because there's no way they would have let Eve continue a relationship with him. I can only imagine how quickly they would have put an end to the two of them seeing each other.

My sister was sneaky, I'll give her that. She was easily the most paranoid person I've ever met, so to be targeted by Mya and Gareth and get roped into their business blows my mind.

But keeping Alex out of the house, keeping any proof of him off Eve's phone, making sure they only met out of town —it all makes sense now. She had to keep him as hidden as possible.

"I know, Alex." I'm doing my best to keep my voice calm, but the entire time I'm on the phone with him, I'm looking around my bedroom, trying to find anything that might be out of place. I have no proof Mya was here other than I can feel she was. "And I'm sorry I didn't bring this up to you sooner, but I don't think I can do this."

"Can't do this?" There's a hollow note in his voice, a tone I haven't heard yet. It makes me stop looking around the room and sit down on the edge of the bed so I can talk to him properly. "That's the best you can do, Eve? You can't do this?"

My mouth is dry. If I knew how this conversation was going to go, then there's no way I would have picked up. I would have ignored his call. But if I had, not only would I not know that he wasn't ever supposed to come over to the house, but I also wouldn't have learned that Mya had been here.

Not that ignorance is bliss, but it has to be better than what I'm feeling right now.

"Well, let me tell you something that I can't do, Eve. I can't ignore the evidence in front of me."

I freeze. The only movement I feel is my pulse. It's slow and steady, thrumming through me like bass music that's too loud. "What do you mean, Alex?"

"Detective Lee thinks Millie should still be in prison for killing your husband, but I've been doing some digging to see if I can find the real killer, and I'm not so sure that he's right. From where I'm sitting, Millie appears pretty innocent, but someone else doesn't."

I'm faint. My vision gets cloudy. I close my eyes, count to ten, then open them again. Nothing has changed. I still have the phone pressed up against my ear; I still need to figure out what to do about Alex.

"Alex, what are you saying?" My lips are dry; I lick them, ignoring the fact that my entire mouth is dry.

"I'm saying that there's a lot of evidence out there that needs fresh eyes on it, Eve. I can be those eyes, or I can make sure other people don't get to look at it. I can do that for you, but only if you let me."

"What evidence?" Eve would know exactly what Alex is talking about, but as soon as the words are past my lips, I realize that I asked the wrong question.

"That's what you're worried about, not that there are people who would love nothing more than to look into that evidence? Geez, Eve, I have no idea what's gotten into you right now. I want to protect you, but I can't do that if you don't want to be with me. Why would I?"

My heart slams in my chest, and even though I feel like I'm drowning, I force myself to take a deep breath. Right now, I'm not even concerned with trying to be Eve. I should be pretending to be my sister so Alex doesn't get suspicious, but that thought is the furthest thing from my mind.

All I want to do right now is figure out what Alex knows or doesn't know. The evidence that might show my sister's guilt was never given to me, for obvious reasons. Sure, the police looked at her as a possible suspect, but her alibi held firm, and I didn't have one, making it clear to them as well as anyone following the trial that I was the murderer.

But Alex makes it sound as if there's a lot more to what's going on. He's making it seem like I need to pay attention because he has some bit of information that could do Eve in.

And right now, I'm Eve.

I'm very interested in what he has to say.

"I'm sorry," I hear myself saying. "Alex, you're right. I think we should get together and talk. There's no way that the two of us can work this out without being face-to-face." I say the words and close my eyes, hoping that he'll bite.

"You want me to come over now?" There's surprise in his voice. Frustration. I hear the emotions, but I'm not entirely sure what to make of them.

"Now's great," I lie. What I want to do is get in that safe and see what Mya changed. I want to examine the house bit by bit to see what Mya did, if anything.

"Eve, you know I'm changing shifts. I told you that already, and that's why I wanted to come by before I headed in to work. I can't be there now because I'll be working, but I'll come over tomorrow afternoon."

I exhale hard. "Sounds great, Alex, thank you."

Thank you for what? Blackmailing me into dating you?

There's too much of that going on right now. Too much blackmail, too many people knowing more about my sister than I ever did.

I'll see Alex tomorrow, and this will end.

33

MILLIE

SUNDAY

The house is clean. Immaculate even.

It's like nobody lives here, or the person who does is obsessed with cleaning up after themselves. Eve obviously was, and I admit I like keeping it as clean as she did. I wipe down the counters one more time, pull a batch of cinnamon rolls from the oven, push the door shut with my hip, then put them on the stovetop to cool.

Before prison, before my entire life fell apart, I loved to bake. It's silly to want to get back into it right now, when I feel like I don't have control over anything, but baking takes my mind off the fact that Alex will be here any moment now.

I don't want to consider the idea of evidence existing that will point to Eve as the murderer. It would be fine if she were still alive and I could watch as she went to prison, to face the same hell I did, but she's no longer here. It's not like I can offer her up on a silver platter without admitting what I did, is it?

I highly doubt the court system would take kindly to me taking care of my sister for them. I went to prison for a murder I didn't commit, and there's no way in hell I'm going back there for one that I actually did.

Grabbing a fresh pineapple that I picked up at the market this morning, I center it on a cutting board and slice off the top with the sharpest knife in the kitchen. It sinks easily into the golden flesh; my mouth starts to water when juice pools on the cutting board. Flipping it around, I lop off the bottom and set it on one end. I'm preparing to cut off the skin when the doorbell rings.

I pause, gripping the knife tight, then put it down carefully on the counter. I'm wearing one of Eve's aprons, a frilly black thing with huge pockets in the front for storing cooking utensils, I suppose—although I highly doubt she ever cooked herself. Sure, there was plenty of food in the kitchen when I moved in, but I can't see my sister cooking.

I can see her hiring someone to do it, though. Most of the meals were takeout from various restaurants. I also found some freezer meals that she could easily throw in the oven whenever she got hungry.

I open the door and greet Alex with a smile. His expression is dark. Without waiting for me to invite him in, he pushes past me, stalking straight to the kitchen. I lock the door and follow him without speaking, and watch him pour a drink of whiskey from a bottle in the cupboard above the refrigerator.

I didn't even look up there. What other things does Eve have hidden in this house that I don't know about yet?

He swallows the amber liquid quickly, then pours another drink before finally looking at me. His eyes look haunted. I've seen eyes like that before. I lived with people who looked like he does now, like they've lost all hope in the world. For the longest time that was how I looked when I saw my reflection in the mirror.

"How are you?" I feel the need to say something, do something to break the uncomfortable silence growing between us. "How was your shift last night?"

"The detectives working your husband's murder case were idiots," he finally says, putting the glass down on the counter with a *thunk*. "You know that, don't you? You were glad they were."

"I have no idea what you're talking about," I say, resting my hip against the counter. I'm tired of trying to be someone I'm not, tired of pretending to be Eve when it's clear her life is so exhausting.

"Eve." He runs his hand down his face and sighs. "Honestly, you know how I feel about you. And that I want to do whatever I can to keep you safe. But I can't very well do that if you're not going to be honest with me, can I?"

"I don't know how to be more honest with you."

I feel like I'm sinking. The air in the kitchen is tight. Stifling. Overwhelming. It's how the air felt when I first entered prison. Then, I couldn't shake the feeling that I was never going to get out of there. I have that same feeling now, like I've been backed into a corner and there isn't anything I can do to get out of it.

"Millie didn't kill Joe!" He slams his hand down on the counter hard, the sound ringing in the room.

I jump and take a step back from him.

"You know it. I know it. Thank God the detectives I work with are too damn dumb to figure it out on their own, but they'll get it eventually. You understand that, don't you? You can't hide forever. You can't pretend forever that you weren't involved."

I have no idea what to say. Anything I could say to get him

off my back slips from my mind. I want to argue with him, tell him that I'm totally innocent, because I am. Eve isn't, but never in my life did I think anyone would figure that out.

When I met Alex, I never saw him as a threat. The only problem I thought would arise from my relationship with him was if Mya or Gareth were to find out about him. He's too kind, just a small-town boy looking for love in the wrong place. But now that he knows something he can hold over my head, I'm not sure what he's going to do about it.

"Eve, the evidence is there. The detectives aren't going to connect the dots yet, but they could. I can help you. I'll make sure nobody ever realizes you were involved. But there's one thing you have to do for me."

I don't want to answer him, but as the next word leaves my lips, I realize how in trouble I really am. "What?"

He grins. Just that one word lets him know that he is right about it all.

"I love you, Eve. I love you more than anything in this world, but you're pushing me to do this even though I don't want to. I can save you, but you have to stay with me."

"What?" I shake my head. "You're blackmailing me into staying with you? Are you insane?"

"Not insane." He smiles at me and pats his pocket. "You think that I'd be so stupid as to ask you to do something like that if I didn't have leverage? No, I have something that would send you to prison tonight. I can put it in the evidence box at work, or I can keep it with me. It's your choice."

"What do you have?" I don't want to know, but I also have to find out what power he thinks he has over me. "Alex, what do you have that could do that?"

While I wait for him to respond, I try to think through what it could be. It doesn't make sense for there to be a shred of evidence that could convict Eve. If there was, I wouldn't have gone to prison for her. Unless somehow the evidence was missed. Unless someone kept it back and hid it from the police.

There are too many possibilities of what happened. I can't worry about that right now.

"There was a bug. I have a tape proving everything."

"A tape? They recorded me talking before Joe died?"

He laughs. "No, after. The detectives wanted you hugged because you were a suspect, and I was the one they got to listen to all of your tapes. I fell in love with you then, Eve, and I knew I couldn't hand your tape over and send you to jail. After Millie went to jail for you, I kept it. It's my way of making sure you don't leave me. You were cleared. But you don't have to stay cleared."

"So if I keep dating you, you'll keep that tape out of the evidence box?" I can't believe what I'm saying, can't believe what he's saying. It doesn't make any sense, but here we are.

"I love you!" Keeping one hand on his pocket like he's afraid the tape is going to disappear, he steps closer to me. "Don't you see that, Eve? I love you, and I'll do anything for you. I can't let you go to prison for the crime your sister did. Work with me, and I'll keep people from getting suspicious of you. I'll make sure nobody finds out you were involved. I don't care what you did to Joe. He sounded horrible, and you just need someone to love you. I'm that man. I've loved you since I listened to your tapes, and I know you only did what you had to do. Stay with me, and I'll keep you safe."

"And if I don't?" I stare in horror at the man in front of me. No, I don't know him very well, but this version doesn't mesh with the man I met in the park. He seemed so kind, so loving.

Then again, my sister fell for him, and she's the most twisted person I knew. It was probably insane of me to think he'd be anything but twisted, as well.

"If you don't, I'll take this to the police station right now. I'll slip it into the evidence box, and they'll find it tomorrow.

How quickly do you think you could get out of town before they catch you?" He grins at me.

I take a shuddering breath. "You really want to end it like this?"

He shakes his head. "I don't want to end anything, darling. That's what you don't see. I have a way that we can make this work. You have to stay with me. Trust me. We have a good thing going. This is what I wanted from day one. You keep me at arm's length, Eve, but I don't want that. I want you, and I'll do whatever it takes to have you."

My mind races as I think about what to do. There are dangerous people out there. Hell, I was locked up with a bunch of them for the longest time. I never thought Alex would be one of them.

"I love you," I tell him, noting the way his eyes soften a little. "Let's make this work." With a smile, I walk up to him and lightly touch his arm. "Why don't you go upstairs, and I'll be right there. I want to make sure I turned off the oven."

He kisses me, his mouth hard on mine, and when he pulls away, his look is triumphant. He seems thrilled with himself, thrilled that this worked out the way he wanted.

"I knew you'd come around," he tells me, cupping my cheek.

My skin crawls at his touch, but I don't pull away. Instead, I watch as he smiles at me, then turns and walks toward the stairs.

"Don't be long," he calls from the foyer. "I want to show you how committed to you I am."

"I'll be right there," I call back. My eyes flick around the kitchen as I worry about what to do. As soon as I see the butcher knife I used to cut the pineapple, it hits me. The weapon is heavy in my hand. I slip it into one of the pockets on the front of my apron.

I have to take care of this.

34

MILLIE

SUNDAY

Alex's blood is sticky on my hands. I wipe them on my apron and stand back from him, panting. My hair has fallen loose around my face, and I reach up to fix it, wincing when I smear blood on my cheeks. I'm sweaty, breathing hard, and my ears are ringing.

"What the hell did I do?" I ask, then drop to my knees next to Alex's body. I search his pocket, and when I pull out the tape he brought over as blackmail, I throw it onto the bed to deal with later. Maybe I'll keep it. Maybe I'll listen to it and destroy it. I'm not sure yet; all I know is that I have to get rid of him.

His cell phone and keys are in his other pocket, and I yank them out. I put the keys on the floor next to me before tapping on the phone screen to wake it up and check for messages. Nothing. Nobody has called or texted him recently. There's no way for me to know how long it will be before someone reaches out to him, but I'm going to have to get rid of the phone.

And his car.

"Shit," I mutter, sitting back on my heels.

Alex's car is in the driveway. I have his cell phone, and I have no idea how I'm going to get rid of both of them. It's not like I can leave them here at the house to find when his colleagues come looking for him after he misses his next shift.

This wasn't how any of this was supposed to go. When I met Alex, I thought he was a nice guy. I thought for sure he'd take our breakup well, that he would walk away, that he wouldn't cause a scene. I had no idea that he would react in this way. No idea that he would try to blackmail me into staying with him rather than let me go.

"Okay, Alex," I say, putting my fingers against his neck to feel for a pulse. He's still warm, his skin soft under my touch. I wince when I press my fingers harder into his neck.

Nothing.

Exhaling with relief, I look him over. When I killed Eve, she was downstairs. It was hard enough to get her out of the house and bury her without anyone seeing me, but now I'm going to have to drag Alex down a flight of stairs and out the back door, to the woods. For the second time since getting out of prison, I'm grateful my sister has so few neighbors overlooking her house, allowing me to move around the property without the worry of someone seeing me.

It takes a long time to get Alex's body to the top of the stairs because I have to run out to the garage to find a tarp I wrap him in so he doesn't bleed everywhere. By the time I get him down the stairs, I'm sweating. I take off the apron and tie my hair up into a ponytail before I move again. I want to get him out of the house and through the backyard into the woods; then I can start digging the hole.

I make it.

The shovel handle feels rough in my hands as I sink the blade into the ground. I scoop up dirt and tip it to the side. I'm well aware that Eve is in the ground just a few feet from me, but I keep my back to her grave, working quickly to toss the soil onto a growing pile. I feel an urgency growing, a need to move faster. Not only because I'm losing daylight but also because the possibility of Mya or Gareth coming to check on me without warning scares me.

I finish the hole.

"In you go," I say, unrolling the tarp and pushing against Alex's back until his body falls into the grave. He lands on his side, his face twisted up as if he's trying to say something to me. I stand up and toss in the first shovelful of dirt.

Then something hits me.

I know how to get out of this.

I stop what I'm doing.

With my mind racing, I run back into the house. Slowing down long enough to kick off my shoes, I head upstairs. I need to keep everything as clean as possible. The last thing I want is for Gareth or Mya to be able to tell what I've done.

My heart beats so loud as I open the safe, I can hear it in my ears. The tapestry presses heavily on my back. I finally pull the door open and step inside the room, my eyes sweeping over every item stored neatly on the shelves.

"I need something that will tie this to Gareth," I say, tracing my fingers over the piles of money and bottles of pills. My fingerprints are on some of them. I skip those, not wanting to bury anything with the body that might tie me to the murder. "There has to be something I can bury in the grave with Alex that will incriminate Gareth."

Then I see it. There's a single pistol tucked behind an empty backpack on the second shelf. It could be Mya's. I chew my lip as I consider if it's a risk I'm willing to take. I want a guarantee that it's Gareth's, but there's no way I can be sure.

I just know that I haven't touched it, and chances are good that Gareth's fingerprints will be on the weapon. I've never seen Mya carry a gun—although I wouldn't put it past her if push came to shove. Still, this is the best option I have.

Backing out of the safe, I grab a T-shirt from the bedroom and return, then use the cloth to pick up the gun, making sure I don't touch the gun.

"Don't drop it," I mutter to myself as I hurry back down the stairs, slip on my shoes, and head out the door to the backyard. It's much darker outside now, and I wish I could turn on the back light to see better, but I don't want to attract any attention. I cut through the backyard around the side of the house to the woods. Across the street I see the glow of a neighbor's front porch light. The door slams, and I freeze, waiting.

Nobody calls out. I don't hear anyone move, so I do, and I'm finally at the grave. Bending down, I reach in and put the gun in the grave. I pause. Should I put money or drugs in there, too? How much can I take from the safe without Gareth or Mya realizing what I did? It's not like the two of them check the safe religiously to make sure nothing is missing, but surely they'd notice, right?

It doesn't matter. I'm running scared.

Never in my life have I felt this out of control, this unable to stop and think things through. Before I can think things through, I've run back up to the house, collected more items, and dumped three bottles of pills and a wad of cash on top of Alex's body.

"Move it, Millie," I whisper to myself, grabbing the shovel and covering him up with dirt. The only light now is from the moon, but it's not full. I have to move carefully so I don't trip as I work my way around the grave, tamping the dirt down with my feet. The smell of fresh dirt is sharp in my nose as I cover the grave with leaves, moving faster now as I dump and scatter them to try to make the grave blend in with the rest of the ground.

Just like Eve's.

The tarp and shovel go back in the garage. I'm a mess, but I'm still not finished.

Tomorrow I'll come out here and double-check that the grave doesn't look obvious. Now, I have to get rid of the car and the cell phone. Steeling myself for what I'm about to do, I shower quickly and change into fresh clothes before grabbing Alex's cell phone and keys.

At the last second, I pick up Eve's driver's license and debit card and slide them into my pocket. The last thing I want is to run into problems and not be able to take care of myself.

The drive across town in Alex's car takes no time since the streets are mostly empty. After pulling up to the river that runs along the park, I park the car and carefully wipe down the steering wheel before doing the same to the door handle. Every noise behind me makes me turn and look over my shoulder, but I'm the only one here.

I still need to hurry.

When the car is as clean as I think I can make it, I throw the keys and the phone into the river, then rub my hands up and down my arms to try to warm up. It took fifteen minutes to drive here, and the last thing I want to do is walk home, but I don't have much of a choice.

I'm halfway down the street, moving quickly and keeping my head down, when my phone rings.

35

MYA

SUNDAY

"Where are you, Millie? You know that you're supposed to be at home at all times so I can come by and get in the safe without having to let myself in. And where the hell are you? I have no idea. Not here, that's for sure."

It's chilly out, and I stamp my feet, moving in a circle under Millie's porch light while I look around the neighborhood. The houses here are lit up, soft lights glow in the windows, but I don't see anyone moving around inside.

"I had something to do. An errand." Millie sounds out of breath on the phone. "You can let yourself in, or it can wait." She also sounds frustrated.

"That's not the point. The point, Millie, is that you're supposed to be here when we need you, when we want you. And what kind of errand did you go on that didn't require your car?"

I already checked in the garage on the off chance that she might be hiding in the house and refusing to answer the door. At first, that's what I thought she was doing when I saw her car inside, but she's not that reckless to ignore me. Millie might not want to play the same games that Gareth and I make her play, but I have a good feeling she's going to try, because she knows the other option isn't nearly as good.

Hiding in the house and pretending I'm not outside ringing her doorbell doesn't seem like something she would do, if I'm being honest.

"I had something I needed to do." Millie's short with me, and I don't like it. I also don't like the idea of her doing something without getting it sanctioned by me or Gareth. "I'll be home shortly."

"Where are you?"

Pulling my keys from my pocket, I turn around and walk to my car. It growls to life immediately, and I back out of her driveway, whip out of the cul-de-sac, preparing to head for her.

"Millie, where?"

There's a slight pause, and I imagine her trying to decide whether or not to come clean with me. She doesn't want to, that much is obvious, but it's chilly out and dark, and wherever she is, she doesn't have her car. Just when I'm about to ask her again, to get my point across that she needs to answer me so we can get this mess straightened out, she speaks.

"The corner of Kanuga and Fifth," she says with a sigh. "I'll wait under the streetlight."

After I hang up on her, I swear, then press down on the gas, driving as quickly as I dare. It's not that I like Millie. In fact, I wouldn't have thought it possible to dislike someone more than I did Eve, but I do. I'm not going to save her because I enjoy her company. I'm going to pick her up and get her back home because she's our investment.

That's all.

Gareth and I need her to fly under the radar so we don't ever have to worry about her grabbing the attention of the police. The last thing we need is for her to get picked up by a cop while she's wandering around alone in the dark, and have it come back to us. I doubt that it would, but the best way to make sure something doesn't come back to hurt you is to take care of it in the first place.

The streets are empty, the night too dark for people to be walking around alone. I make good time in my drive across town.

A scowling Millie's standing right where she told me she would be. I pull up next to her. She throws open the car door and slips into the passenger seat. Then she slams the door and glares at me before she speaks.

"Thank you."

She says the words, but she doesn't mean them, and I can tell that they hurt her to say.

"What were you doing?" I ask her, pulling away from the curb. Now that I'm sure she's safe, I can drive a little slower. I don't have to worry about something bad happening to her. I don't have to worry about the police picking her up and getting involved. The lower the risk of her getting on an officer's radar, the better off we'll all be.

Gareth and I have plans for this eventuality, of course. We both know it's entirely possible that she'll get a speeding ticket, or think that she can blab to someone about what's going on. That would be a nightmare.

While it wouldn't be the end of the world, Gareth and I don't want the stress of setting up a new safe in someone else's house. We don't want to have to start the blackmail process all over again. Eve fell into our lap, and Millie is another lucky stroke for the two of us.

"I told you. An errand."

Slamming on the brakes, I bring the car to a screeching halt in the middle of the road. "Millie, I swear to God, you'd better start talking and tell me why you were out here without your car in the middle of the night. It'd better be a very good explanation because I'm going to pass it right along to Gareth."

She doesn't flinch. Her jaw is tight, and I can see her pulse beating in her neck. When she glances at me, her expression is so dark that it's impossible to see any compassion in her eyes.

But I do see something.

If we weren't next to a streetlamp, there's no way I would have noticed the smudge on her cheek, almost in her hair-line. It's dark and small, but I've seen enough blood in my life to know exactly what it is. My mouth drops open as I reach out and brush her hair back from her face.

"Why the hell do you have blood on you?" As soon as I ask the question, though, I already have my answer. "Who did you kill, Millie?"

She shrugs; the movement is so casual compared to what's been going on out here that it's almost laughable.

"Millie, who the hell did you kill? I need you to tell me so I can help you cover your tracks."

This is the absolute worst-case scenario that I can think of right now. Sure, I know she killed her sister, but I didn't think that we'd run into this trouble again. Anger rips through me while I wait for Millie to answer.

Outside, there isn't anyone around. Everyone else has gone home to bed, which means that nobody cares that I stopped in the middle of the road, my car taking up an entire lane.

"It was a cop," she finally says, looking me right in the eyes.

"You killed a cop?" She can't be serious.

Millie scoffs. "Eve was dating him," she says, her voice soft. Low. Dangerous. "Eve was dating him, and he was getting too close. He had information that would put her in prison for Joe's murder. I have it now, and I killed him."

"You're joking."

I press the green call button to call Gareth. He needs to hear this. This isn't something I can relay to him later, when the sun is up and things still don't make sense. I need him to know exactly what's going on so we can figure out what to do about it together.

Millie takes a deep breath when Gareth answers; his voice fills the car.

"Mya, is there a problem?"

I clear my throat and hold the phone out between Millie and myself.

"Millie has something to tell you," I say.

Millie smiles. "I killed a cop, Gareth," she says. She's speaking to him, but her eyes are still locked on me. She refuses to look away from me even as I meet her stare. I don't want to be the one to break it first.

"You did what?" His voice is low. Full of danger.

"I killed him, and I buried him with your gun. Your drugs. Your money."

My mouth falls open. Millie didn't mention this to me. Killing someone is bad enough, but making sure that she buried him with incriminating evidence that would end up putting Gareth in prison if we weren't careful?

I honestly can't believe it.

Neither can Gareth, judging by the silence on the other end of the line.

He clears his throat, breaking the silence. "I swear to God, Millie, if this is a joke—"

"It's not. He'll be reported missing tomorrow. Alex Johnson. Watch the news." She smirks at me. "Thanks for the ride."

I should stop her from getting out of the car. I should stop her from walking away and doing God-knows-what, but I can't seem to lift my hand or raise my voice. I feel stuck in my seat right now. Millie slams the car door and walks quickly down the sidewalk. Her head is up, and she's scanning her surroundings. Her hands are shoved in her pockets.

"Mya, tell me she's lying." Gareth is livid. I hear it in his voice.

I swallow hard before answering, "I don't think she is." Millie turns the corner and disappears from my sight. "She's serious, Gareth. What are we going to do?"

My mind races as I try to think about how we're going to handle this, how we're going to put the lid back on this disaster. Millie is clearly determined to blow the entire thing out of the water.

"We have to stop her," he says.

I nod even though he can't see me.

"You need to find out if she's telling the truth about this officer. Find her. Find out where she buried the body."

"Alex," I murmur. "I can't find out the truth until tomorrow, until it hits the news. It's not like I can call around to the police department to ask if he's gone missing. But I'll follow her, Gareth. I won't lose sight of her."

I hang up on him and press down on the gas pedal. The car jerks forward, and I drive to the corner where I saw Millie turn. My headlights cut across the sidewalk and empty buildings, the light reflecting back from the windows.

She's gone.

36

MILLIE

SUNDAY

My back is cold from pressing it against a brick building in the alley I'm in. When I see headlights shine down the road, I don't dare move.

Mya is looking for me. Of course she is. The last thing I wanted was for her to make me get back in the car, for her to make me answer questions. I needed to get away from her before she became angry enough to try to hurt me.

"What did you do?" I ask myself, sinking down to the ground. I balance on the balls of my feet, unwilling to sit down on the ground where a puddle of goo gathers at my feet. Still, my legs feel weak, and I know I'm not going to be able to stand for much longer.

I have to figure out what I'm going to do.

It was one thing for me to kill Alex to keep him from blackmailing me, but another thing entirely to blackmail Gareth.

That might possibly be the stupidest thing I've ever done.

Under the pale moonlight, I hold my hands out and search them for any sign of what I did. No blood under the fingernails, no proof that I murdered a cop. I scrubbed them clean in the shower, the same as after I killed Eve.

"Oh, God," I say, grabbing the sides of my head. "Oh, God, okay."

Exhaling hard, I stand up and walk to the end of the alley, looking both ways to check the road. Mya's gone, but that doesn't mean I won't run into her again. I don't think that she and Gareth would kill me, not when I haven't told them where Alex's body is, or if I'm bluffing, but she might.

I hurry down the sidewalk, jumping at every sound I hear. I'm almost home, and what I want to do now is get inside, lock the door, and take another hot shower. I want to pretend this never happened, but I know full well what's waiting for me at home.

Blood. Cleanup. It's contained upstairs, but I still need to clean it up before Mya or Gareth see it.

There are smears of blood on the floor where I killed Alex, but at least the tarp did a great job keeping the rest of the house clean. If Mya gets there first, she might snoop in the woods and find the grave. Once that happens, I'm sunk. The two of them not knowing where the grave is located is the only thing that's keeping me alive right now.

The thought spurs me into a run. There's a stitch in my side, and I do my best to ignore it, relying instead on the adrenaline that's been pumping through my veins all evening. I'm sucking in air, and I have to stop and walk multiple times, but finally I turn onto the street where I live.

Eve's house—my house—is at the end of the street, and I pause for a moment before walking past my neighbors' houses. All are dark and silent, like sleeping sentries sitting on hills that are back from the road. Even if someone was awake and peering out their front window, I highly doubt they'd be able to see me moving along on the road.

But my house is a different story. The front porch light is on, but so are the upstairs lights. They shine from the windows, and I pause at the mailbox, wondering if I left them on by accident. That's more than enough to attract attention from my nosy neighbors if anyone wakes up to see them.

Halfway up the driveway, I realize I'm not alone. Mya's car is parked off to the side, tucked partially under the shade of an oak tree, making it almost impossible for me to see it there. I hesitate, suddenly unsure of what to do.

This entire night I've been acting on autopilot. I did what I needed to do to survive without much giving thought to whether it was the right thing to do. Switching that up now and trying to think things through is difficult, when the only thing I want is to lock myself in the safety of my house.

But I swallow hard, reminding myself that my house isn't safe. Not really. Not when Mya and Gareth are inside. I might think that I can hide away in my house and they won't be able to get to me, but that's not true—the lights on upstairs in my house prove that.

For a moment, I think about running again. I don't have my car key. Without my car I don't have a way to get far from here, but I'm not opposed to trying, to put as much distance as possible between me and Mya and Gareth.

But where would I go? No matter the destination, people would notice that Eve is missing, and that would mean the cops would look for her. Mya and Gareth might come clean with the fact that I'm the one who killed her. Or maybe they wouldn't, but the end result is the same.

Someone, somewhere, would find me. They'd find out I'm not Eve, and then I'd be locked up forever for killing her.

"I can't go back to prison," I whisper.

All I've done since my release has been to keep me from

getting locked up again. I keep running into the same problem—I can't seem to get free.

I managed to get freed from prison; then I got locked back up by Mya and Gareth. Just when I thought things might be working out, Alex decided to blackmail me, too.

I groan, bending over and grabbing my thighs, as I breathe through my nose and try to keep from throwing up. If I go back into that house, I'm not sure what I'm going to find. Mya is in there, that much is obvious, but what is she doing? Will she kill me? Will she try to hurt me for making her life that much more difficult?

"Shit," I mutter, running one hand across my forehead. I'm sweaty, my skin is prickly and uncomfortable, and I can't seem to shake the dread. "I don't know what to do."

I can't continue to stand out here on the driveway. I'm lucky that my neighbors haven't noticed anything strange going on over here yet, but I can't rely on that luck holding out. I have to keep moving.

Even though I don't want to go inside the house, I don't see how I have much of a choice. My feet feel heavy as I climb the steps to the porch. The door is closed but unlocked, and it opens silently when I turn the knob.

Inside the dark house, I blink hard, looking around.

I see a figure standing next to the staircase.

I'm not sure how this is going to go.

37

MILLIE

SUNDAY

Gareth leans against the ground-floor banister, his arms folded across his chest, a scowl on his face. He's angrier than I've ever seen him. His cheeks and neck are splotchy and red; his eyes are dark, his nostrils flared.

When I don't reply immediately, he rolls his head, cracking his neck, then fixes me in place with his stare.

"What did you do?"

I shiver as his words wash over me but don't immediately answer. Mya must have picked him up on her way here since that's her car outside, but that doesn't tell me where she is. Upstairs, probably.

I look past him into the other rooms, trying to find any proof that she's in the house, but I don't see any movement.

Whatever she's doing, wherever she is, she's being quiet.

"I need coffee," I say, ignoring Gareth and heading to the

kitchen. It's insane to turn my back on him right now, but chances are good he's going to follow. He wants answers—needs answers—so I'm not surprised when I hear his footsteps behind me.

It sends a shiver up my spine to know he's behind me and I can't see what he's doing, but I don't turn around. Instead, I busy myself with the coffeemaker, dumping in more grounds than necessary. Right now, I need my coffee to have legs, because I feel like I'm about to collapse on the floor.

When it's finished brewing, I pour myself a mug and doctor it up with cream and sugar, then drain half of it. I finally look at him. He's standing by the counter now, his arms still crossed. My eyes flick to his hips, but I don't see any sign of a gun there.

That doesn't mean anything. He sometimes wears it tucked into the back of his pants. There's no way he'd come to my house with everything going on and not bring something for protection, I'm sure of it.

"What you just told me is very upsetting," he finally says. "Look me in the eyes and tell me whether or not it's true."

There's a soft *thunk* above our heads. I look up at the ceiling before answering, "Mya's in the safe."

He nods. "What did you do, Millie?"

"I protected myself."

I take another sip of coffee. It's too hot, even with the cream, but I like how the scald makes me feel something. The rest of my body feels numb. I honestly can't believe what happened here, and I need something to make me feel alive.

Grounded. I need to feel grounded so I can think this through.

Gareth is smart, but I want to walk away from this. To do that, I need to be smarter.

He still hasn't responded, so I refill my mug and grip it

tightly. Steam swirls up into my face. It's so hot it's almost painful, and I breathe it in.

"Millie, I need to know if it's true. Did you really kill a cop?"

I nod once, and his entire expression changes to disbelief. Gareth scrubs a hand down his face. He looks unsure of what to do with me. Shaking his head, he pins me in place with his stare. "You killed a cop. Where's the body?"

"I can't tell you that. It's my insurance."

"Insurance?"

I nod, knowing full well that he understands it's black-mail. He knows I buried Alex with a gun, drugs, and money that will hopefully tie to him. He just doesn't know where I did it.

"You wanted insurance against me."

I nod again. "Wouldn't you?" I take a tiny sip of my coffee, but instantly regret it. It scalds the tip of my tongue, and I wince, unable to ignore the pain.

"Where's the body, Millie? Mya said she picked you up on the far side of town. You obviously drove the guy's car away, didn't you? You dumped the body somewhere, buried it, hid my things with it, and now you have to hope that nobody will ever find it. Am I right?"

Instead of answering, I stare at him.

He pushes away from the island and takes a few steps toward me. "Where did you bury the cop, Millie?"

"You know what I can do right now, don't you?" I ask, ignoring his question. "I can go to the cops. I can tell them what you did, that I think you hurt him, that you two are evil people. They're going to start looking for him soon anyway, I'm sure of it, but they'll ramp up their search efforts. They'll do anything to find him and bring him home, and when they do, they'll find your things."

I don't tell Gareth that Alex is buried on this property. I

can't tell him he's buried next to my sister. That's something I should have thought through better, but I can't change it now. I can't back down. I have to keep pushing this, make sure he sees that I will do anything to protect myself.

Instead of looking threatened, instead of acting worried by what I'm saying to him, Gareth smiles and takes a step closer to me.

It's the same terrifying smile I've seen him use a dozen times when he's upset with me, but it shows confidence that he's going to get his way no matter what I try to do. It makes my stomach drop.

Before I can say something to make it clear I'm not afraid of him, he speaks.

"You should have thought this through better, Millie. You want to play with the big dogs? You threaten someone like me and think that I'll let you get away with it?" He chuckles; the sound sends a tremor of fear through my core. "That's not how this works."

"What the hell are you talking about?" I don't want to believe what's happening, don't want to believe Gareth would turn on me like this, not when I have something to hang him with. "You don't scare me any longer, Gareth. You know as well as I do that if you hurt me, I'll tell."

"You can't tell if you're dead. Mya doesn't get that, Millie. She thinks that we need to keep you happy to make sure you don't turn on us, but she's wrong." He's almost completely closed the gap between the two of us when he lunges at me, his arms outstretched.

In this moment, time seems to stop. I have no idea what I need to do, but standing here will only end up with me dead. I swing my arm out from my body, acting on impulse, and throw the steaming contents in my mug into his face.

"Dammit!" he swears, his voice louder than it has been this entire time.

I barely have time to register that the footsteps above us are now on the move. Mya is headed towards the stairs. Gareth lunges at me, and I fling myself to the side to get out of his way.

He slams into the counter, and I turn away from him, reaching my hand out. My fingers brush against the handle of a knife in the knife block. The entire thing tips forward when he grabs me by the waist and pulls me back.

"No!" With a shriek, I kick back at him, then lunge again for one of the knives. He's yelling at me, his huge hands pawing my body in his attempt to keep me from escaping from him. I continue to struggle and kick, finally throwing myself far enough forward to grab a knife.

As soon as my hand closes on the handle, I feel relief flood through my body.

I'm going to be okay.

Gareth flips me over. His face is bright red, burned by my coffee. His eyes are slits as he stares at me. He's going to kill me.

Before he can get his hands around my throat, I bring the knife up. Once, twice, again and again. I sob as arterial blood sprays onto my face and arms.

The sounds coming from him aren't human, but he lets go of me long enough for me to kick away from him. With my legs shaking, I manage to stand. I feel weak and close to falling over, but I turn from him, my arms already pumping as I prepare to run.

Mya's there.

Her face is frozen in horror, anger etched across it. I look from her face to her hands, which are positioned above her head, holding something. Before I can get out of the way, she brings the object down. The pressure of the blow sends pain exploding through my temple. It drops me to the floor.

38

MILLIE

SUNDAY

God, my head hurts. It throbs, the worst headache I've ever had. Even though my eyes are closed, with the dark pressing in around my body and giving me comfort, I still feel my teeth rattle together. All the bones in my body are screaming in pain, and my muscles ache from being cramped up and still.

I feel like I need to move, like I should run, like I need to stretch out and get away from here, but it's so cozy where I am with my eyes closed. There's a gentle movement that reminds me of being in a hammock. I slowly drift off to sleep.

Then something brushes against my cheek, hard and cold like plastic. I reach up to brush it away. If I can get comfortable, I can lie here and get the rest I need after such a long day. I can ignore the pain pulsing in my body, and the way my head feels like someone has it in a vise.

I just have to push the plastic away, get it off my cheek. It's making a crinkling sound when I move, and that's driving me nuts.

My eyes fly open, and I press my palms up and away from my body. Panic tightens my throat. I claw at whatever is wrapped around me like a cocoon. I'm not in bed. I'm not wrapped in a soft blanket and being lulled to sleep in a rocking chair.

The plastic crinkles under my touch, and even though it's too dark to see what it is, I know exactly what makes that sound.

"No," I whisper, my voice strangled; the sound slips from my lips. "No, no, no!"

My voice is louder now, even though there's another in my head screaming at me that I need to shut up, that I need to stay as quiet as possible, because the one person who might hear me is the wrong person to hear me.

I scrabble at the tarp, looking for a way to unwrap it from my body. It's tight around me. I bend my knees in an effort to loosen it up so that I can try to wiggle free.

The pounding in my head is worse. It feels like someone took a jackhammer to the side of my skull. I grit my teeth, pushing against the pain the best I can. My head feels close to splitting in half, making it so I can't catch my breath. The pain isn't pure and bright, the way it is when you cut your hand on a sharp blade, but dark and murky. It's the type of pain that will pull you down under it and drown you if you let it.

I suck in air and smell plastic and dirt. The combination makes me want to throw up. Breathing through my mouth, I keep pushing; tears stream down my cheeks now while I try to find an end to the tarp.

I have to get out of here.

"Come on!" I kick up, trying to wiggle around enough to break free. As soon as my feet collide with the trunk's roof, though, I stop.

Mya is going to hear me. It kills me to be quiet, to keep from slamming around in the trunk, but that's what I have to do.

I finally find the edge of the tarp. Working my arm out under it, I pull it back from my face and gasp in the fresh air. It's stifling in the trunk, where there's not much air, but it still feels good to be breathing without something touching my face.

I'm being jostled about, and even without being able to see much of anything at all, I can easily tell that I'm in Mya's car. Reaching up, I run my hands along the metal roof, swearing softly to myself.

It's all coming together.

I stabbed Gareth, but only because I didn't have a choice in the matter. There was no way I was walking away from that encounter alive if I hadn't taken extreme measures to stop him. And then I saw Mya, but only for a moment.

Then there was the pain.

Extreme pain. It was so crushing, so overwhelming that I must have passed out. That explains why my head hurts now; the pain is still so severe, the movement of the car is enough to make me nauseous. Turning, I try to angle my body, to feel around for anything that might be useful to get out. And that's when I see it.

The glow-in-the-dark handle.

It's right there to my left, tucked farther back in the trunk than I am. How many times did I notice the one in my car whenever I got groceries out? I knew what it was in the same way that one knows what doorstops are in their house.

But I never knew that it glowed in the dark.

My legs are still tightly wrapped in the tarp, and I shimmy, pressing my palms down next to my body in an effort to angle back. I need to grab that emergency handle, need to yank it.

My fingers brush against it the first time I try to grab it. I swear when I miss, doing my best to keep my voice low.

The second time the same thing happens. I'm almost able to tug the handle, but my grip slips off it at the last second. Grunting, I push myself up and forward again, and this time I grab it. My fingers tighten around it before the handle can slip from my grasp. I yank down hard, putting everything I have into the effort.

I feel a click more than hear it, and then the trunk flies open, bouncing with the movement of the car. Kicking and sitting up, I grab the tarp and yank it off my legs. Cool night-time air hits me in the face, and I feel more awake than I did a moment ago.

Mya hits the brakes, and I go from taking deep lungfuls of refreshing air to being slammed into the floor of the trunk. My head spins when I hit it, and I groan, then push off the crinkly tarp to swing one leg over the edge of the trunk.

She's at a complete stop now, and I take advantage of that by getting out of the trunk. My legs are wobbly and weak, and I almost pitch forward, but I catch myself at the last second by bracing my hands on the car. Above me, fingers of light stretch across the sky. Morning is coming.

How long was I unconscious?

"Millie!"

Mya's voice reaches my ears. I spin away from the car, panic choking me as I try to run. My legs are cramped from being curled up in the trunk. Blistering pain burns up my calves when I put one foot in front of the other.

"Millie! Get back here!" Her voice is an angry hiss, and I'm afraid to turn around and look at her.

I have to keep going.

Each breath only allows a snatch of air to reach my lungs. They burn, like I'm caught in a burning building and can't breathe deeply without drawing the flames into my chest. The edges of my vision blur, and I shake my head to clear it.

The movement sends me sprawling.

Concrete meets the palms of my hands, but the pain is barely noticeable. I feel grit work its way under my skin, but I don't care. I'm too focused on what will happen if I don't run.

I need help. Someone has to drive by, has to see what's going on.

Someone has to stop.

Nobody else is on the road. Nobody is coming to help.

Behind me, I hear Mya getting closer. I have no idea what she's going to do to me. I only know that I have to get away from her or I'm dead. She'll never let me walk away from this. Never.

I bump into something. It must be the curb. I grab it and try to haul myself to my feet. My body screams at me to stay down, to hide, but I can't hide here, not in the middle of the road. Not when she's right behind me, sauntering up to me like she has all the time in the world.

"Where did you think you were going to go, Millie?"

There's so much anger in Mya's voice that I want to shrink away from it. I would give anything in the world to hide from her, to keep her from ever being able to find me again, but I can't do that.

It's just the two of us. On this empty road. The sky slowly lightens, and the day breaks, as if nothing terrible is going on.

Mya leans over me. She's not close enough for me to feel her body heat or her breath, but she's right there. She's not going to back off until she has me.

She's going to kill me.

"What the hell?" Her voice is angry. Surprised.

I want to turn my head to see what she's looking at, but it hurts too badly. A soft whirring sound fills my ears, and even though I want to see what's coming for me, my eyes flutter shut.

39

MILLIE

MONDAY

When I close my eyes, the silence around me is so oppressive that it hurts. Little by little I peel them open, taking my time to adjust to the light before I try to look around me.

There's a soft beeping. The shuffle of feet on the floor. Someone clears their throat, and I wince for the blow, knowing full well that if it's Mya, I don't stand a chance of making it out of here in one piece.

Wherever here is, anyway.

"You're awake, Eve." A woman's voice fills my ears, blocking out the beeping sound. It's gentle and kind, and I turn towards it, finally opening my eyes fully.

Not Mya. Mya doesn't sound that kind, isn't that kind.

Whoever just spoke called me Eve, and Mya calls me Millie, like she enjoys lording the fact over me that she knows who I am.

Blinking hard, I finally take in the woman who is talking to me.

She's younger than me, with a youthful, round face, and she's wearing scrubs. Her stethoscope is slung around her neck, and she has a chart in her hand that she glances at before putting it down on the table by the bed.

I'm in a bed. Not only that, but I'm in a hospital bed, which means I'm in a hospital. What I want to know, though, is how.

My voice cracks, and my mouth feels dry.

"How?" Lifting one hand, I gesture weakly at the room to get my point across.

"You got lucky, that's how." The woman smiles at me. "There was a couple out bicycling this morning, and they found you in the middle of the road, covered in blood. Looks like it all came from your head wound."

My head wound. Where Mya hit me. There's no way for this woman to tell at a glance that most of the blood soaked into my clothes and spattered on my cheeks wasn't mine.

I swallow hard. "Who?"

She shakes her head, the smile still on her face. "They didn't leave their names, didn't want anyone to know who they were. Good Samaritan types. But they brought you here, and that's what matters in the end, isn't it? We were able to get you changed into clothes and found your driver's license in your pocket. That's how we figured out who you are, Eve."

"I want to go home." It's frustrating to be flat on my back talking to this doctor. I grab the side rail of the bed to pull myself up.

She rushes to my side, puts her arm around my back and helps me up so I'm sitting.

"There you are, Eve. I know you want to go home, darling, but you can't right now. Not until we check you out and are confident that you're okay. You came in with quite the head injury, and we did an MRI, but we still want to monitor you. You needed fluids, the whole nine yards."

I shake my head, but that movement makes me feel sick. "I'm Millie, not Eve." She has to believe me, has to listen to what I'm trying to tell her.

"You've been through a lot of trauma, Eve." The doctor smiles at me, fine lines appearing around her eyes when she does. "It makes sense that you are a little confused."

Anger boils in me, and I have to tamp it down to keep it from reaching the surface. "I'm not confused," I say in a clipped tone. "I feel better than ever. I'm Millie. My *sister* is Eve."

There's a pause, and I think for a moment that I'm getting through to her, but then her mouth tightens. The expression on her face is that of a disappointed grandmother. I hate how she looks like she feels bad for me.

"Eve, you had your driver's license and debit card in your pocket. We know who you are." Her volume drops a little bit, and she reaches out to pat my hand. I'm too stunned to try to pull it back from her. "We know about your sister, about her going to jail and then getting out. Nobody would be able to handle the pressure you've been under."

"You've got it wrong. I'm Millie."

She's silent, watching me. "This isn't the first time you woke up, Eve, but it's the first time you've stayed awake. You kept telling the nurse you were Millie."

"I am." Swallowing hard, I stare at her, trying to make her see that I'm telling the truth. "I'm Millie."

She sighs, and the sound crashes down on me.

"I hope you'll understand why we wanted to call in a consult. In times like this, it really is the best option to get a professional to come see what they think needs to be done. We want to do what's best for you."

I blink at her. "Consult?" The word feels unfamiliar in my mouth. "What do you mean? I want to go home."

Home. I'm suddenly reminded of what's waiting for me at Eve's house. There's blood upstairs and on the stairs where I dragged Alex outside to bury him. There's the safe full of illegal things that I'm sure could get me locked away for a long time if someone were to find them.

There's Gareth's body. My stomach clenches when I remember him on the kitchen floor. I remember him coming for me, remember the fear I felt over the worry that he was going to kill me.

Looking away from the doctor, I take a deep breath, then another.

I have to get that visual image out of my head.

"Eve," the doctor says gently, reaching out and putting her hand on my shoulder. The action makes me look up at her. "We want what's best for you here, and right now to get that means calling in someone to help. You've been through a lot of trauma."

"I'm not Eve," I whisper.

The smile doesn't leave her face. "Our psychiatrist will be here shortly, Eve. I want you to meet with her, okay? Just talk to her. She'll be able to help you figure out what's the best option for you. Until recently, you couldn't tell us anything about what happened to you, and the last thing we want is to rush your treatment or send you home if you're not ready."

"I am ready, though." She obviously doesn't believe me, but maybe she doesn't have to. Maybe I'll swing my legs over the side of the bed and get out of here on my own. She can't stop me. Nobody can stop me.

I'll call a cab. She mentioned having my license and debit card. I'll use them to get out of here. I have to go to Eve's house to get my things, but then I'll skip town. Becoming Eve seemed like the perfect idea when I had it—the easiest way to finally enjoy the life I deserved after spending so many years in prison for something I didn't do.

The doctor must see the look on my face because she closes her eyes for a moment. She holds up her hands between the two of us. "I have to tell you, Eve, that if you try to leave without being discharged by the psychiatrist, we will hold you here to make sure you get the treatment you deserve."

"What?" I stare at her, looking for any sign that she might be joking. "You've got to be kidding. There's no way you can do that to me! I didn't do anything wrong. I want to go home." Tears stream down my face. I feel them, cool against my hot skin, but I'm too busy gripping the bars of the bed and staring at the doctor to think about wiping them away.

"The psychiatrist will be here soon." Her voice is soothing, calm, obviously designed to make me trust her. I can only imagine how many patients she uses it on in a day. The mental image comes to me of her standing in front of a mirror at home, practicing her look to make sure it's as calming as possible. I shake my head to get rid of it.

"Seeing things you don't want to, Eve? I hope you can understand that this is the reason why we need to keep you here. We need to make sure you're going to be okay in the long run. Physically, you're fine. Your head needs longer to heal, and you might have problems with dizziness, but we have medication for that. We can take care of that." She tilts her head as if to make sure everything she's saying is getting through to me.

"Then I'm fine. Let me go. You're right, I'm Eve. I made a mistake." I smile at her. Her face is blurry through my tears.

"That will be up to Dr. Patterson to decide. She should be here soon, Eve. Don't go anywhere." She walks out the door. I watch her leave, my heart beating hard.

I'm going to make a run for it. I will. I just have to wait

long enough for her to get out of here, for her to lose sight of my room. When she doesn't immediately leave my line of sight, though, I stiffen. My whole body goes tight when I see her talking to someone in the hall.

"She thinks she's her sister," the doctor says, keeping her voice low. "I told her that she had to stay here and talk to you to make sure she was okay. She was pretty upset about it. I'm not sure how much you're going to get out of her in her current state."

"Don't you worry. I'll take care of her," the other person says.

Do I recognize her voice? I strain and lean forward on the bed. My eyes close as I try to focus on who the doctor might be talking to.

"You're the expert, but I don't think there's any way she's ready to go home. Not when she's this delusional. She hit her head hard, and it may be from that, or it could be from stress." The doctor sounds worried, like she really cares.

That doesn't matter to me. What matters is getting out of here.

"It might." There's that voice again. I swear I've heard it before.

My head aches, tight and painful, and I can't seem to focus on the sound of the woman's voice to tell who she is.

The woman I can't see continues. "But there's always the unfortunate chance that the damage is more permanent. You can trust me, Dr. Jones. I'll take care of her."

"I appreciate you coming in. I know you were off call, but it means a lot that you showed up this early on a Monday. It's clear your expertise is needed here."

"My patients always come first. Have a good morning."

There's silence; then I hear footsteps moving down the hall. Opening my eyes, I stare at the door, willing whoever is in the hall to stay out there. I don't want to see who's going to walk through it in a moment.

There's a slight pause. The sound of high heels hit the tile floor. The person from the hall steps through the door. She grins at me like we're long-lost best friends.

"No." I don't even have the energy to scream.

EPILOGUE

MYA

LATER

My high heels click as I walk down the hall. There are some people who find it annoying when women do that, they think we're showing off, and they're right.

I am.

I'm feeling lighter than I have in days. Weeks. *Months.* It's not every day that you get to take revenge on the person who ruined your life. It's not every day that you get to have complete power over someone who would love to grind you into the dirt.

It's not every day you get to ruin the person who killed the man you love.

But that's exactly what I've got.

I pull my badge on the lanyard around my neck out and hold it out to the scanner at the door, wait for the beep, then let myself in. The psych ward is locked for a number of reasons. It's designed to make sure family can't come and go and upset patients without proper approval, but it's also great for making sure nobody can leave without permission.

Like Millie. She wants to leave. She keeps crying about leaving. But she won't ever leave, because I'll never give her my permission.

Glancing down at my badge, I can't help but smile when I see my image grinning up at me. Dr. Mya Patterson, MD.

It worked out fine in the end, didn't it? I loved Gareth and would do anything for the man. I would have followed him to the ends of the earth if it meant that I got to spend time with him. He was funny and smart and driven in a way that I've never seen in another man.

So when he told me about the side business he had selling drugs, I offered to help. It was easy to get my hands on certain prescriptions when he asked me for them. It was easy to get the drugs out of the hospital and pass to him to sell. And once we were able to blackmail Eve into helping us, everything got a whole lot easier.

Then Millie took him from me, and now I'm never going to let her go.

As I pop into my office to check my schedule for the day, my mind wanders back to how we ended up here. That's something I haven't fully explained to Millie yet, how it all worked. And I want to. I want her to look at me and know that I'm the reason she's here, the reason she's never going to get out. I want her to realize that everything she did, all the murder and lying, it all led to here.

A knock on my door makes me look up. Tiffy, one of the girls who handles the patients, leans in. She's got full, round cheeks and is always smiling, but that will stop soon enough. She's fairly new here, but nobody smiles on this ward for long.

"Eve Overstreet is ready for you. I have her in a room for

your appointment with her, but she's under supervision, don't worry."

"How's she doing today?" I grab my notebook and a pen while I wait for Tiffy to respond.

She shrugs. "Not great. Of course you'll take another look at her medication to make sure it's the right dose and type, but I wanted to tell you that she keeps claiming she's not Eve. She's going on and on about being Millie, about Eve being dead, about everyone being dead."

I nod. *That simply can't continue.* "Thank you for letting me know. It's a tragic case."

Tiffy murmurs in agreement. "I didn't live here when Millie murdered her sister's husband, but my boyfriend filled me in. No wonder Eve went off the deep end." She looks at me guiltily, like she just realized what she said. "Sorry about that."

"Not a problem, I understand. It can be frustrating, but I love what I do."

The police were certain to go back through the evidence box to see if they missed something and pin Joe's murder on Eve, but I got rid of the tape I found in her bedroom after I listened to it. Her boyfriend, Alex, must have stolen it from the evidence room and brought it to her to show her that he knew the truth. None of that matters anymore, though. Alex is gone, Gareth is buried, the tape is destroyed, and the house is clean.

I'm sure the police would love to ask Eve and Alex questions, but they'll have a hard time finding her wherever Millie buried them. I also have no doubt that officers will come to the hospital at some point to try to talk to Millie.

That's why I'm happy to do what I must to keep her quiet.

My heels click even louder as I walk to the small room where Millie is waiting for me. She glances up when I open the door and step inside. Her face falls when she sees it's me.

Tiffy is right. Her medication isn't where I want it yet. She's still able to recognize me and show so much emotion, but I'll take care of that.

"How are you feeling today?" I ask, avoiding calling her by name. Calling her Eve sets her off, and even though I love doing that, I need to get her medication adjusted so she doesn't cause a problem.

"I'm not Eve." Millie stares at me and plants her hands on the table between us. It's bolted to the floor, as are the chairs. There's nothing loose in here that she could use to hurt herself or hurt me. In the corner there's a camera, the red light blinking to remind me that someone is watching.

Nobody is allowed to listen in, because that would break confidentiality, but if she becomes violent, someone will step in to stop her.

Flipping open my notebook, I make a show of scribbling in it like I'm actually taking notes. "Do you remember who I am?"

She glares at me but doesn't speak.

Good. She doesn't remember me, although it's obvious she remembers how she feels about me. Still, I like knowing that she has no idea who I am. She can hate me all she wants, a number of my patients do.

"Millie," I say, locking eyes with her while I use her real name, "I'm worried about you. I think that you're confused about who you are and why you're here, and I want to help you with that. Would you like to know the whole story?"

She nods, and I lean forward.

"After you killed your sister, you killed her boyfriend. He had proof that Eve was the murderer, didn't he? You had to get rid of him." My voice is so quiet that she has to lean forward to meet me halfway. We're both leaning across the table, but I'm still far enough away that she can't get to me. Not yet.

She doesn't move. Her mouth is parted slightly, and she's barely breathing, watching me like she's afraid to look away, in case I do something to hurt her.

"You then killed my boyfriend. Gareth." I like saying his name. I like reminding her of whom she killed, although it's not like she's going to remember for very long.

A flash of recognition appears in her eyes. "Gareth," she says, rolling the name around on her tongue like it's a piece of candy. "You and Gareth did this."

I nod. "You went to prison for a long time, Millie, but you didn't deserve to be there, did you?"

She shakes her head.

"But you deserve to be here." I could call the cops and let them know what Millie did. She killed three people, and I'm sure they'd love to send her back to prison for that, but she could point the finger at me, and I can't let that happen.

Besides, if she were to leave me, who would I have fun with every week?

There's just one question I need answered, one loose end I have to worry about. "Millie, how did Alex get the tape? Where did it come from?" I destroyed the one copy of it, but there could be another.

Someone out there could know the truth about what happened. It gives me chills to think about. I don't like the idea of anyone coming for Millie thinking she's Eve, but I have a way to handle that. I'll keep her drugged, make sure she never makes sense.

No matter what happens, I'm not letting her out of my sight.

"Tape?" She sounds confused.

Useless. It was folly of me to think she might have any information that could help me. Leaning back in my chair, I make a show of looking at the notes I brought in with me. It's time to end this meeting, make sure nobody can ever get any information out of her.

As for the tape, the copy I found in her room is destroyed. I have to hope there isn't another copy of it out there. Allowing her to be lucid enough so she can talk to me about it would risk her figuring out what I'm doing to her.

It's not worth it.

"I'm changing your medication," I tell her. "Today. We want to make you as happy as possible, Eve."

There. That will set her off. It does, and she stands up, slamming her hands on the table. "I'm not Eve!" She screams the words, then points at me. "You did this! You did this to me!" Her voice is loud and clear, and I wouldn't be surprised if the staff heard her from outside the closed door.

"Eve, you need to calm down." I stand up and back up to the door. The camera can't see me, can't see the grin on my face, but I look like I'm in danger.

"I'm not Eve!" She runs at me, but the door bursts open, and two men grab her. I see one man holding a syringe. He waits until the other grabs her and holds her steady before plunging it into her arm.

"Are you okay?" The man with the syringe says to me as he depresses the contents.

"I'm fine." My cheeks are flushed, but out of excitement, not fear. "Thank you for coming in."

"That's why we watch the camera." He points up to it like I don't know it's there. "We'll get her into her room."

"I need to change her medication," I say, my voice rueful as I shake my head. "It obviously isn't the right dose yet."

As they carry her out of the room, I head toward my office, ready to write her a new prescription. By the time she wakes up, it'll be ready to go. I'll make everything stronger so I don't have to worry about her remembering something and spilling the truth.

Not that anyone around here is inclined to believe her, but it's still not worth the risk. I don't want her running her mouth off, telling even the tiniest snippets of truth about me and how I was involved with her prior to her coming to the hospital. Besides, if the police ever try to talk to her, I have to make sure they won't get anything coherent out of her.

"Dr. Patterson, do you have a moment?" Tiffy appears at my side. Her smile has faded a little bit, and she's wringing her hands.

"Of course. What can I do for you?"

She leans forward. "There are police officers here. They want to talk to Eve about a missing man they think she may have been involved with."

"Oh, dear." I tap my finger against my chin to make it look like I'm thinking. In reality, I knew this day would come. I knew I might have to prepare for this, and I am.

"I'll come talk to them, but they're going to have to understand that she's simply not able to talk. She's completely delusional all the time, and now that she's violent, I've had no choice but to increase her medication." I shrug, like none of this can be helped.

But it can. I could change everything, could end this hell for Millie in a moment. I could free her from this prison.

But why would I ever want to?

THANK YOU FOR READING

Did you enjoy reading *Her Perfect Life*? Please consider leaving a review on Amazon. Your review will help other readers to discover the novel.

ABOUT THE AUTHOR

Emily Shiner always dreamed of becoming an author but first served her time as a banker and a teacher. After a lifetime of devouring stacks of thrillers, she decided to try her hand at writing them herself. Now she gets to live out her dream of writing novels and sharing her stories with people around the world. She lives in the Appalachian Mountains and loves hiking with her husband, daughter, and their two dogs.

ALSO BY EMILY SHINER

The Secret Wife

The Promise

The Caretaker

Her Perfect Life

The Stolen Child

I'm Following You

You Can't Hide

Her Husband's Secret

The Better Mother

Made in the USA
Las Vegas, NV
11 May 2025

21981408R00152